BETWEEN THE TOWANS

Finding Love Where the Towans Meet the Sea

Bren Moore

KDP

Copyright © 2025 Bren Moore

All rights reserved

The characters and events portrayed in this book are fictitious. Any similarity to real persons, living or dead, is coincidental and not intended by the author.

No part of this book may be reproduced, or stored in a retrieval system, or transmitted in any form or by any means, electronic, mechanical, photocopying, recording, or otherwise, without express written permission of the publisher.

To Ron & Joyce and Cyril & Iris - gone but never forgotten.
This book is written for you.
With Love, always,
Bren

CONTENTS

Title Page
Copyright
Dedication
CHAPTER 1: Sand in the Sheets — 3
CHAPTER 2: The Quiet Hours. — 8
CHAPTER 3: The Edge of the Map — 12
CHAPTER 4: Keeping Distance — 16
CHAPTER 5: Morning Rhythms. — 20
CHAPTER 6: Sunday Light. — 24
CHAPTER 7: Driftwood. — 29
CHAPTER 8: London Lights. — 35
CHAPTER 9: The Unexpected Gift. — 41
CHAPTER 10: Call of the Ocean. — 45
CHAPTER 11: Between the Dunes. — 49
CHAPTER 12: Shorelines — 53
CHAPTER 13. The Quiet Shift. — 59
CHAPTER 14: Smoke and Light. — 64
CHAPTER 15: Familiar Strangers. — 67
CHAPTER 16: Saltwater Light. — 72

CHAPTER 17: The Morning After.	77
CHAPTER 18: Something Else Entirely.	80
CHAPTER 19: The Click of the Shutter.	84
CHAPTER 20: A Little off Centre.	88
CHAPTER 21: Cracks in the Silence.	92
CHAPTER 22: Ask Me Anything.	97
CHAPTER 23: Scratching the Surface.	101
CHAPTER 24: The Drive Back.	105
CHAPTER 25: Bruised Edges.	110
CHAPTER 26: Linen and Thorns.	113
CHAPTER 27: Salted Truths.	116
CHAPTER 28: The Space Between.	120
CHAPTER 29: What the Tide Brings In.	124
CHAPTER 30: All the Right Reasons.	128
CHAPTER 31: Finding Love Between the Towans.	132
Acknowledgement	137

Between the Towans
Bren Moore

CHAPTER 1: SAND IN THE SHEETS

Iris

The wind had been up all night, rattling the thin lodge windows and hissing through the dune grasses like it had something urgent to say. But by morning, it had softened — tamed, almost — as if it had said its piece and now wanted only to drift.

Iris Nansloe stood barefoot on the wooden decking of Sea Breeze, Lodge Five, cradling a chipped mug of instant coffee. Her damp auburn hair clung to her neck in loose curls, still tinged with salt from her morning bodyboard. She liked to get into the sea early, before the tourists arrived with their windbreaks and cool boxes and Bluetooth speakers, before the beach turned from sacred to spectacle. Just her and the water and the steady beat of her heart as the waves lifted and spun her, reminding her she still existed in something larger than linen changes and biscuit trays.

Behind her, the bed she'd just made was picture-perfect — white duvet fluffed, pillows stacked with precision, the wool throw folded just so across the end. It looked untouched, a showroom lie, though she knew by sunset it would be kicked to chaos by whoever had booked the weekend. She didn't mind. It was the rhythm of the job. Comfort in repetition. Clean, replace, smooth, erase.

She bent to scratch behind the ears of Moss, her faithful chocolate Labrador, who was sprawled in a sun patch just outside the door, his tongue lolling, his paws caked in yesterday's sand. He groaned appreciatively, eyes half-closed, ears flicking lazily against the morning breeze. He was greying now — around the snout, especially — but still loyal as ever, equal parts stoic and shameless scavenger. It was often hard to tell whether his eyes were soulful or just scheming for crumbs.

"Five more to go," she murmured. Moss gave a dramatic sigh in reply, stretching his back legs and blinking like a dog who'd much rather be napping than supervising laundry.

The Dune Lodges were marketed as 'eco-luxury retreats nestled between Gwithian Towans and the vast Hayle estuary.' To Iris, they were simply work — a row of glass-and-wood boxes perched among the dunes like polished shells, filled with other people's prosecco-fizzed weekends and filtered Instagram lives. She liked the quiet guests best: couples who arrived with books and left the loungers exactly where they found them. No trail of sand across the floorboards, no half-unpacked beach bags or sticky-fingered toddlers smearing jam on the fridge handles. She could get in and out in twenty minutes with those. Still, the lodge names amused her: Beach Retreat, Ocean Drift, Salt & Sky, Dune Light, Tide Watch. Aspirational, soothing, slightly smug. Cheryl — clipboard queen from the London office who hadn't touched real sand in five years — insisted on calling them "wellness sanctuaries." Iris just called them Tuesday.

She didn't resent the work. It paid the rent on her little weather-beaten cottage tucked behind the dunes, kept Moss fed and herself grounded. There was peace in motion — washing, folding, replenishing. It left no room for overthinking, which suited her most days. What it didn't do, however, was leave space for anything else. Not really. Not art. Not connection. Not risk.

She drained the last of her coffee, reapplied a smudge of suncream across the bridge of her freckled nose, and slipped the mug into the dishwasher for the next guest to find clean and soulless. Freckles had always bloomed on her skin the moment the sun touched it — a scattershot inheritance from her mother, who used to call them "sun kisses." Iris had spent her twenties trying to cover them up with tinted moisturisers and too much self-consciousness. Now she let them be. They didn't make her invisible. Just more herself.

With a soft whistle, she signalled Moss, who stood with a creak of ageing joints and shook himself from nose to tail, his collar tags jingling like distant bells. Together they crossed the raised boardwalk toward Beach Retreat, her cleaning tote swinging at her side, filled with fresh linens and sprays that all smelled vaguely of lemon and hotel soap — clean, forgettable, and trying a little too hard.

Halfway across the sand-blown path, something caught her eye — a glint of soft light where it shouldn't be. She crouched and brushed aside a dusting of sand to reveal a small, pale green piece of sea glass, smoothed by time and tide, no sharp edges left to betray its origin. She held it up to the light. It glowed like a captured memory, blurred at the edges, impossible to place but deeply familiar.

"Nice," she said aloud, and slid it into her pocket, where three others already nestled: a frosted white shard shaped like a leaf, a cobalt sliver like an eyelid, and an amber chip that reminded her of the colour of the tea her gran used to brew in a proper pot. She never went looking for them. They simply turned up, as if they knew where they were meant to be. Just like Moss, just like this life — not quite planned, not entirely chosen, but somehow hers.

Later, when the day's beds were made and towels stacked in tight rolls, she'd tip the glass onto her workbench at home, alongside driftwood and feathers and broken shells she'd collected without thinking. Some pieces she arranged into picture frames or mirror borders. Others sat for weeks in little bowls, waiting to tell her what they wanted to be. It was instinctive, untrained — not art, not really. At least not in the way people meant when they said art.

She'd never shown it to anyone. Never dared. Her ex, Nate, had once picked up one of her frames and turned it over like it might be harbouring something dangerous. "It's pretty," he'd said with a flat, amused smile. "But you're not seriously thinking of selling this sort of stuff, are you? People buy real art, Iris. Not bits of glued junk."

She'd laughed at the time, played it off. Said no, of course not. It was just a hobby. Something to pass the evenings. She'd stopped showing him anything after that. Stopped making, too — for a while. But over the last year, something had shifted. Quietly, like the tide turning under a new moon. She'd started again. Just in small bursts, when the house was quiet and Moss was snoring, and the weight of being unseen grew too heavy to ignore.

Maybe it wasn't art. Maybe it was just fragments and glue. But it felt real to her. And sometimes, just sometimes, she wondered what it would feel like to show someone — the right someone — and not hear laughter or see indifference in their eyes. Someone who'd look and see. But that was dangerous thinking.

Moss bumped against her knee with a soft grunt, as if to say, Are we doing this or what? She stood, brushing sand from her knees. "Right. Onward. Crumbs await." And together they moved toward the next lodge, the light already rising higher, the day beginning again in salt and silence and small, beautiful pieces.

CHAPTER 2: THE QUIET HOURS.

Iris

The last lodge was always the longest. By the time Iris had stripped the beds, wiped down the counters, and repacked the welcome basket at Tide Watch, the sun had begun its slow, golden slide behind the dunes. The air, once warm and briny, had cooled into something quieter — an evening hush that only really happened near the sea, as if the coastline itself was exhaling.

She walked the path home with Moss trotting a few lazy steps ahead, stopping now and then to sniff at tussocks of sea thrift or the ghost of a crab shell. Her back ached slightly, a dull pull between the shoulder blades, but she didn't mind. The walk soothed her — wind in her hair, sand still in her shoes, the everyday beauty of the Cornish light pressing gently against the edges of her thoughts.

Her cottage, nestled into the shoulder of a dune, came into view. Towans Reach, a name carved into an old slate slab at the gate, barely visible now beneath lichen and time. Built in the 1920s, it had once been a summer escape for her grandparents — a modest place with flaking blue shutters, thick stone walls, and a roof that always needed patching somewhere. It had been passed down over three generations, weathered and wobbly in places, but still standing. Still hers.

They'd been farmers, both of them — Ronald and Joyce, from a small inland village in South East Cornwall. Their lives had been ruled by fields, animals, and early starts, and yet they'd dreamed of sea air. Not to leave farming behind, but to balance it. Every year, they'd head west to the coast when the season allowed, and here on this edge of the dunes, they found the stretch of sky they'd been craving.

Ronald had built the place with his brother just after the war — floorboards creaking, windows uneven, but sturdy enough to last. Joyce planted the first sweet peas against the side wall. Together, they returned each summer, bringing simple joy with them — jam sandwiches, folded deckchairs, a radio with a bent aerial. In the old letters Iris had found tied with string in a biscuit tin, they wrote to each other like lovers always returning. Their love wasn't grand or performative — it was quiet, practical, rooted in shared work and held silences. It lasted.

She pushed open the gate and followed the winding path of flat stones, the garden wild and defiant around her — lavender leaning out across the gravel, mint escaping its pots, daisies cropping up in places she hadn't planted. Moss slipped through the door ahead of her, already curling up on the mat like he was claiming the warmth before she could.

Inside, the air was cool and familiar. She kicked off her shoes and went straight to the small living room, its mismatched furniture softened by throws and cushions faded from years of sun. A row of black-and-white photographs lined the mantelpiece — Ronald and Joyce, frozen in laughter, in seaside clothes, in the act of simply being. Ronald with his sleeves rolled to the elbow, Joyce with wind-swept hair and the kind of smile that didn't need perfect teeth to be beautiful. Iris always paused here. Always let herself feel it.

She changed into softer clothes — a worn cotton dress, bare feet on flagstone floors — and made tea in the old enamel pot her gran had used for decades. It still whistled when it was ready, as if it had something to say. In the corner, Moss gave a long, satisfied sigh and flopped onto his side, belly exposed. He was getting on now, slower to rise in the mornings, but he was still her shadow. Still her boy.

The window above her workbench let in the last of the evening light. She pulled up the rickety stool and tipped out her finds from the day — sea glass, a few shell fragments, a twist of dried seaweed with elegant lines. They clinked softly as they fell onto the wooden tray she used for sorting. Each piece had its own weight, its own shape, like it was carrying a secret the tide didn't want to keep.

She reached for the frame she'd started earlier in the week, laying out the glass and shells slowly. No plan. Just instinct.

It wasn't art, not in the gallery sense. No training, no big ideas. Just pieces of what the sea gave back, rearranged until something inside her clicked.

Once, years ago, she'd shown a frame to Nate. He'd picked it up, turned it over like he was looking for a barcode, and said, "It's sweet. Bit crafty, though, isn't it? Like something you'd see at a church fête." He meant it kindly, she thought. Or at least without malice. But she hadn't shown him another.

Still, the work had crept back in over time. Quietly, like damp under the door. When the lodges were silent, when Moss was asleep and her mind wouldn't settle, she found herself sorting through colour and shape, letting her hands do what they needed to. She never expected anything from it. She didn't show it, didn't sell it. It was hers, and it was enough.

Outside, the light dipped lower. The garden swayed in the breeze. Somewhere down at the lodges, a door closed for the night, and the clink of wine glasses echoed faintly in the distance. She didn't look. She set the unfinished frame on the windowsill, where the last light caught the pale green glass and made it glow. Then she sat for a while, tea cooling beside her, her fingers dusty with salt and glue. Thinking of Joyce. Of Ronald. Of that kind of love — patient, weathered, sure of itself. A kind that didn't shout. A kind that lasted.

Sometimes she wondered if such a thing could still exist. And sometimes, more often than she admitted, she quietly hoped.

CHAPTER 3: THE EDGE OF THE MAP

Rafi

By the time he turned off the A30, Rafi could feel the edges of his body again — stiff from too many hours gripping the wheel, his jaw tight from the kind of clenching that creeps up on you slowly, until you realise you've been holding everything in place just to keep going. The road had narrowed into something unmarked, more suggestion than route, winding past hedgerows that scraped the sides of the Land Rover like brambles tugging at old thoughts.

The air changed out here. Less exhaust, more salt. More space between things. He wound the window down and let it in, the smell of seaweed and wild grass drifting through like something remembered rather than newly discovered.

He hadn't told anyone where he was going. Just said he was "taking some time." As if that meant anything anymore. As if the people asking cared beyond the shape of the headline or the click of the next message thread. He hadn't even told Jules. She'd get it, eventually. Or maybe she wouldn't. Either way, he needed to disappear for a while. Maybe longer.

Cornwall had felt far enough. Not dramatic, not tropical, not overly poetic. Just far. A place where the land runs out, and the sea takes over — and maybe, if you're lucky, you stop needing to explain yourself.

The sat nav had stopped trying about ten minutes ago, confidently declaring he'd arrived while he was still looking at cows and a dead end. That was fine. He didn't need digital certainty. He had the email printed out — Ocean Drift, Lodge Eight. Key in lock box. No reception. No contact unless necessary. That last part had sold him, more than anything else. Privacy wasn't a luxury these days. It was survival.

The gravel beneath the tyres shifted as he turned into the Dune Lodges entrance — a weathered sign, a strip of decking barely visible beyond the dune grasses. The place was smarter than he remembered. He'd been here once, years ago, on assignment. Brief. Functional. He couldn't even remember the name of the man he'd photographed — someone who shaped surfboards and talked about saltwater like it was sacred. Rafi remembered the light, though. That particular pale gold you only get in places close to the edge of something.

The lodge came into view — modern, clean-lined, all glass and pale wood, with a name etched onto brushed steel by the door: Ocean Drift. A bit much, but it would do. He cut the engine and sat there for a moment, not moving. The only sound was the ticking of the engine cooling and the faint whisper of the sea over the dunes. That sound always did something to him. Stripped things back.

He climbed out slowly, shoulders tight, his back stiff from the drive. The wind hit him full in the face, and he stood there, letting it. No one else around. No voice calling his name. No stranger watching from a window. Just the gulls circling high above and the long grass flickering like flames across the dunes.

The lock box was tucked into the side rail of the decking, basic and black, with a four-digit code he'd already memorised. He punched it in, opened it, took out the single key tagged Lodge Eight, and let himself in.

The place was spotless. Too spotless. A showroom pretending to be a home. It smelled like citrus and cedar, but beneath that, there was something colder — the kind of scent that comes from a space nobody's lived in properly. He dropped his bag by the door and stepped through to the back of the lodge, unlocking the sliding glass doors and stepping out onto the deck.

There it was. The reason he'd come. The sea, just beyond the rise. He couldn't quite see the water from here — the dunes were too high — but he could feel it. Hear it, under everything. That low, rhythmic breath of something older than anything he'd brought with him. It steadied him, a little. Or maybe it just drowned out the other noise — the looping thoughts, the things unsaid, the headlines and half-truths and the weight of being watched.

He leaned against the rail and let the wind move through him. It was sharp, full of salt, bracing enough to sting, but he didn't pull away. He welcomed the discomfort. It reminded him he still had edges.

He pulled the camera out of his bag without really thinking. Reflex. Muscle memory. The strap curled easily into his hand, the weight familiar. He lifted it, adjusted the focus, and framed the edge of the dune, a ribbon of light cutting across the grass. There were footprints leading away from the nearest boardwalk — not his. Not recent. A curve of someone else's life, already moving away. He pressed the shutter. The click felt too loud in the stillness. He checked the frame, then paused. Not this time.

He deleted the photo. Not out of frustration — but because he didn't want to keep anything just yet. He wasn't here to document. He wasn't even sure he was here to remember. He just needed to be somewhere where no one was watching. Somewhere he didn't have to be the man everyone else expected. Somewhere he could unspool quietly, privately, without having to explain.

He closed the camera case and leaned back against the rail, the sun now low enough to flatten the shadows. Maybe here, at the edge of the map, he could finally stop moving. Or maybe he could finally start again.

CHAPTER 4: KEEPING DISTANCE

Rafi

He'd slept, but not well. The bed was too soft, the silence too complete. The kind of silence that didn't feel peaceful but vacuumed-out, like a sealed room with the air slowly thinning. He'd turned the pillow over twice before giving up and lying there in the dark, staring at the ceiling while the lodge creaked and settled around him — not in a familiar way, but like it was adjusting to him, tolerating his presence the way people did when they recognised him in airports or cafés. Cordial. Impersonal. Too much space between the words.

In London, there was always sound. Cars, late-night deliveries, someone arguing three floors down, the low hum of the underground like a pulse beneath the city. Here, there was none of that. Only the hiss of dune grass shifting in the wind and the occasional crack of the wooden deck as it cooled in the dark. He thought the quiet would bring him peace — that in losing the noise, he might lose the weight of it all too — but instead, it left a vacuum where the thoughts settled heavier, like dust in still air.

The next morning was bright, and falsely hopeful. The kind of light that promised a fresh start, though Rafi didn't trust it. The kettle in the lodge was too clean, the tea too bland, and everything he touched seemed designed to look good on a brochure, not to be used by a person with tired hands. The mugs were white and smooth and soulless. The teaspoons matched each other. It all made him feel like a trespasser in a life that didn't fit.

He walked for an hour instead, the dunes spilling out toward the beach like something half-remembered. The sea was a blurred line in the distance, and he didn't go near it yet. Just traced its edge with slow steps, letting the wind take some of the heat from his chest. He hadn't lifted his camera once. Not because he didn't see anything worth capturing, but because the idea of taking felt wrong. Like photographing a house you didn't live in.

By the time he got back, the sun was sharp through the floor-to-ceiling windows, the deck already warm beneath his boots. He'd just kicked them off when there was a knock at the glass door — soft, hesitant, and completely unwelcome. His hands stopped moving. He'd been promised no interruptions. It was the first thing he'd asked for, and the only thing he'd insisted on. No check-ins, no friendly touches, no one knocking to ask if the temperature was to his liking or if he'd like to book a massage. Cheryl had confirmed it herself, voice brisk and bored on the phone — No interruptions, Rafi. Just you, the dunes, and whatever it is you're running from.

So when he moved toward the glass door, every muscle was braced. She was standing on the deck, barefoot, wind pulling strands of hair loose from a messy braid. She wasn't smiling, but she wasn't uncertain either. She held a bundle of white linen in both arms and nodded when she saw him approach.

"Hi," she said, her voice muffled slightly by the glass. "Sorry — just the spare pillowcases. I forgot to leave them yesterday."

He opened the door only as far as necessary.

"I was told there wouldn't be anyone."

Her expression didn't change. "I know. Cheryl said the same. This was my mistake. I didn't want it to look like we'd missed something."

Her tone wasn't defensive. Just efficient. Tired, maybe, but not apologetic in the way he expected. She handed the linen over without fuss, without small talk, and turned to go before he could say anything else.

Her dog — a large, greying Labrador — trailed behind her with the solemn gait of an old soldier. It didn't look at him. Just followed her, as if they'd both done this a hundred times before.

He watched them go, because it was the only thing he could do. She moved quickly, like someone who didn't want to linger but didn't care enough to hurry either. And for a moment, just before she stepped off the decking, the light hit her — caught in her hair, in the pale line of her shoulders, in the way her eyes, when they glanced back briefly, were the colour of cold water. Clear and deep and disinterested.

He closed the door harder than he meant to. Dropped the linen onto the arm of the sofa and exhaled slowly through his teeth. He was annoyed. Not shaken. Not intrigued. Just irritated — that she'd come at all, that the one rule he'd asked for had been broken so casually, and that now her face — that sudden, uninvited moment — was lodged in his head like grit under a lens.

This was supposed to be a retreat. A place where he could go unseen and unspoken to. Not a place where barefoot women with windburnt cheeks and tired eyes wandered up to the glass like it was nothing. He didn't care who she was. And he didn't want to care that he'd noticed her at all. He was here to forget. Not to notice.

CHAPTER 5: MORNING RHYTHMS.

Iris

Mornings had a rhythm, and Iris liked to keep to it. She rose early, sometimes before the light had fully crept across the dunes, and took Moss down to the beach while the tide was still low and the sand cool underfoot. It was never crowded that early. Just a few dog walkers, the odd runner, and the sea — always the sea, vast and calm and barely touched by sound. She didn't need to swim or board every morning. Some days, just walking beside it was enough. A reassurance. A reset.

Back at Towans Reach, she'd put the kettle on while hanging the towels out in the garden, the pegs clutched in her teeth as she folded and clipped and smoothed each one along the line. The sun was already warming the air, softening the scent of salt and grass, and Moss flopped into his usual patch of shade, content with his short patrol. There was a comfort in repetition — tasks that asked little of her brain, but gave her body something to do. Fold. Wipe. Tuck. Breathe.

She would've had breakfast next — tea and toast, maybe some apple slices, if they weren't already soft in the bowl — except she'd spotted the linen. Two pillowcases folded neatly atop the laundry stack. Still clean. Still waiting to be delivered.

She stared at them for a moment longer than necessary. It wasn't a major mistake. Not the end of the world. But it was unlike her. She took pride in being thorough — not out of perfectionism, but because in a world full of noise and unpredictability, she liked being someone who did the quiet things well.

Lodge Eight. Ocean Drift. The new guest. The one with the note in bold: No interruptions. She hesitated, hand hovering over the linen, knowing that Cheryl would tell her to leave it. Most guests wouldn't notice. Most didn't care. But still, the thought of that blank space in a drawer unsettled her.

She left the cottage without changing shoes, the pillowcases tucked under one arm, Moss following close behind with the slow, heavy pace of a dog who didn't need convincing. The morning had brightened — one of those quiet, hot days where everything shimmered slightly, as though reality were holding its breath. The dunes rolled soft and silent ahead of her, the sky already beginning to bleach at the edges.

She hadn't planned to knock. Just drop the linen and be done. But he'd been there. Right there. Inside the lodge, behind the glass, moving toward the door before she could turn away. No chance to leave unnoticed.

He opened it just enough for the air between them to shift, his expression unreadable, his voice clipped.

"I was told there wouldn't be anyone."

She hadn't flinched. She wasn't one for fussing, or filling silence with too many words. Just said her piece, offered the linen, stepped back. No eye roll. No smile. Just something even and neutral — like the rest of her work. He took the bundle from her without touching her hand. Then closed the door. And that should've been the end of it.

Back at the cottage, she rinsed the tea-stained mug she'd left in the sink and poured fresh water into Moss's bowl, watching him drink with his usual theatrics — gulping, snorting, licking the floor around the edges as if it held the flavour he'd missed. The towels snapped softly on the line. A bird called once from the hedgerow and was gone again.

She sat at the table with the second mug of tea, fingers curled around the warmth. It was hard to say what exactly stuck in her. Not his face — that was already blurred. Not his tone — she'd heard worse. Maybe it was just the suddenness of the moment. The jolt of seeing someone when you weren't prepared to be seen. She wasn't used to that. Not here. Not in this life she'd built carefully around not being noticed.

He hadn't looked at her like a person. More like someone who'd stepped into the frame by accident. That shouldn't have mattered. She didn't care what guests thought of her. That was the point — to pass through unnoticed. To leave the beds made and the soap replaced, and not exist in anyone's memory beyond the faint scent of lemon and cotton. But still, there was something in the way he'd looked past her, through her. Like a mirror that refused to hold a reflection.

She took another sip of tea, now lukewarm, and turned toward the workbench. The unfinished frame was still there — sea glass arranged in a curve, pieces waiting to speak. She placed a small shard of pale blue glass near the centre, hesitated, moved it again. Some days she could feel what belonged. Other days, she had to trust that something would tell her, eventually.

It wasn't the guest. It wasn't about him. It wasn't personal. Just one of those small, strange moments that slipped into the shape of a day and made it feel uneven. A slight seam in the quiet.It would pass.

CHAPTER 6: SUNDAY LIGHT.

Iris

It was Sunday. She always knew when it was Sunday. Not because of church bells or alarms — she didn't need those — but because the air was quieter, the wind calmer, and no one in Hayle was in a rush. Officially, it was her day off. Unofficially, she was "available for emergencies," though she had come to learn that the word emergency meant very different things to different people.

Like the time a guest was convinced there was a snake in the shower (a very confused eel left over from a rockpooling expedition), or when a woman rang in tears because her prosecco hadn't been chilled to "spa standard." Once, a couple had called her at 6:45 in the morning because they "couldn't find the sea," which was particularly memorable considering it was, by definition, everywhere.

She kept the work phone charged, more or less, but Sunday

was sacred. Not sacred in the church-and-hymns sense, but sacred in the roast-potatoes-and-carrot-swede-mash sense. Roast day was non-negotiable. First the beach. Then the family. Everything else could wait.

She surfed that morning, taking the long board she rarely used anymore, just because it felt like the kind of day for gliding. The waves were generous — nothing showy, just enough to pull her in and carry her forward like a promise. By the time she returned to Towans Reach, salt clung to her skin, her shoulders were sore in that satisfying way, and Moss was sandy and half-asleep in his usual spot.

She changed, wrapped her hair up in a scarf, and threw on a loose shirt and cut-offs. At her parents' house, lunch was always for 1:30 sharp, though her mum would still be laying forks at 1:45, and her dad would be halfway through carving "just a taste" before anyone had sat down.

Their home sat on a quiet road near the estuary, white-walled with a low stone fence and a garden that was wild in exactly the way Frances claimed was intentional. Her mum opened the door before Iris even knocked.

"There you are," Frances said, already halfway through a sentence. "You've brought pudding, haven't you? Please say you brought pudding. I forgot we'd eaten the treacle tart."

"I brought the crumble you wrapped up for me last week," Iris said, stepping inside and kissing her cheek. "Which I never ate, because I knew this would happen."

"That's why you're my favourite," her mother said, and

added, "Don't tell Tom."

Tom, of course, was already in the kitchen, carving the chicken and dramatically sighing about how no one appreciated the labour he put into "slicing poultry with surgical precision." His wife, Leanne, rolled her eyes and handed him a second bowl for the stuffing. Their three kids — Iris's nieces — were playing a game that involved running in a circle around the table until someone got dizzy or injured. So far, it was a draw.

Lunch was chaos in the best sense. Her dad, Len, had appointed himself wine-pourer, which meant overfilling everyone's glass, then topping them up mid-meal without asking. Frances tutted at the gravy being too thin. Tom passed carrots with a flourish, and Leanne kept asking the youngest — Mae — not to sit on the dog, which Mae did anyway. The roast potatoes were crisp, the parsnips slightly charred, and the love in the room so dense it could have been ladled alongside the gravy.

"Still no boyfriend then?" Tom asked, smirking over his glass.

"Still no indoor voice?" Iris shot back.

"Just checking. You've got this cottage to yourself, ocean views, all that solitude… it's wasted on someone who doesn't even appreciate spooning."

"I appreciate silence," she said, smiling but firm.

"Spoken like a woman who's dated a man who talks

through David Attenborough."

She didn't answer. Just took a sip of wine and looked out the window, where the estuary glittered under a wide stretch of sky. Her mum changed the subject, and the moment passed like mist. But the words sat with her. They always did.

After lunch, they walked the estuary path — all of them, in various combinations, drifting in and out of step. She ended up walking ahead for a while, Moss beside her, the mudflats wide and pale with the tide out. Waders picked through the shallows, and the air smelled of salt and wild thyme. She paused at a familiar bend in the path where the river curled just enough to make you feel like the land had exhaled.

It was perfect, really. The life she had. She knew that. Her work was steady, her family close. She was surrounded by beauty, by space, by the kind of calm most people paid thousands to find for three nights in a hot tub with LED lighting. And yet. Sometimes she felt the shape of absence more than the things she had. She didn't want noise or drama or even the kind of company that needed tending. She'd had that once — someone who'd filled her space like a storm, always restless, always needing more. He'd said her art was charming, once, in the same tone someone might call a child's finger painting 'brave.' He'd talked over her. About her. Around her. Until she stopped offering anything to be heard. She'd ended it. Cleanly. Quietly. But she hadn't invited anyone in since.

Now, she did things her way. Chose her moments. Held

space and let it stay empty, even when it felt like a weight. That emptiness had edges sometimes, but it was hers.

On the way home, she took the long way through the dunes, letting Moss sniff his way back up the trail. The sky was soft with gold. Sea breeze in her hair. That particular stillness of late summer, when everything pauses before the season turns.

She passed Lodge Eight just as the light began to dip, and for a second, she thought the path was empty. Then she saw him. Rafi — the guest — was standing just off the boardwalk, camera in hand, crouched near a cluster of grasses catching the last of the sun. He looked up when she passed, their eyes catching not quite by accident, not quite on purpose.

There was no smile. No nod. Just a glance, flat and unreadable. Then he turned back to whatever he was photographing, and the moment closed. Iris walked on.

By the time she reached her cottage, the kettle was already on in her mind. She opened the door, let Moss in first, and stood for a moment in the soft quiet of her own home — her space, her stillness.

She didn't regret coming back alone. Not quite. But something in her had been stirred. And now, like sea glass, it would take a while to settle.

CHAPTER 7: DRIFTWOOD.

Rafi

The lodge had decent Wi-Fi — better than he expected, actually. Fast enough to stream, upload, even send high-res edits if he'd been that way inclined. He hadn't planned on using it. The whole point of being here was to disconnect — not from the world, necessarily, but from the version of himself that existed inside it. The public one. The curated one. The one with the angles just right and the captions halfway between truth and theatre. But after two nights of watching clouds track the sky like forgotten hours, he gave in. Just a quick check. Habit, really.

He flicked his phone off airplane mode and tapped into the network. The signal came strong, no resistance. Notifications flowed in with casual urgency — messages, emails, a missed call from a gallery in Berlin. A one-line text from Jules: You alive? No punctuation. Just Jules. She always wrote like she was out of breath, even if she never raised her voice. He didn't respond. He wouldn't yet.

Jules had been with him since the beginning. Back when he was shooting derelict train platforms and water-damaged walls in forgotten boroughs. She was the one who'd found his work buried in a student zine, who'd emailed him out of nowhere and said: There's something here. Let's show them. She'd pushed, pulled, protected him. Believed in him harder than he ever had. And for years, it had worked. Until it didn't.

He hadn't told her about Saskia. Or the show in Shoreditch he'd walked out of halfway through, leaving a half-empty wine glass and a full gallery behind him. He hadn't told her he was coming here. Not because he didn't think she'd understand — but because he knew she would, and that somehow made it harder.

He scrolled without meaning to. His thumb moved of its own accord, faster than his thoughts. Until her name appeared.

Saskia Bell.

The latest post was from last night — a gallery event, champagne flutes, ambient lighting, Saskia in black silk and a pose she'd practiced a hundred times. Her caption: "Surround yourself with what inspires you." A man stood next to her, too close to be business. Rafi didn't recognise him. He read the comments anyway. Fire emojis. Hearts. Compliments about her eyes.

He stared at the screen for a moment longer than necessary. Not longing. Not jealousy. Just that weird ache of watching your life carry on without you. He turned off the phone. Placed it face-down on the side table. Sat for a long moment in the stillness.

Then stood. Pulled on a hoodie. Grabbed his camera. He needed air. And light. And things that didn't ask anything from him.

Outside, the wind moved in long strokes across the dunes, brushing the grass like someone smoothing hair. The path to the beach curved soft beneath his feet. He followed it without looking ahead, the lens strap pulling gently at his shoulder.

He used to photograph forgotten places — factories with rusted bolts and flooded cellars, flats with mattresses like fossils of people long gone. He liked what time did to places. How ruin told the truth. In London, the work had shifted — cleaner, sharper, emptier. Commercial. Magazine spreads. Museum commissions. Faces lit in softboxes, filtered down to elegance. He didn't remember when the honesty had left it.

He reached the water without thinking. Rolled his trousers up to the knee. Waded in. The cold was immediate, sharp, purifying — like glass against skin — but it stilled him. It steadied everything inside. The water pulled at his ankles and let go again, like breath.

He stood in the surf, not moving. Not searching. Just letting the weight of things lift slightly. The grief that never quite shaped itself into words. His parents — gone after one of their "let's-make-up-for-Christmas" ski trips. He hadn't gone. He'd said he was working. He wasn't. He just couldn't face the pretending. The photo they sent from the lodge — smiles, scarves, cocoa — was the last one anyone took.

He missed them. Of course he did. But he didn't miss the friction. The constant noise of people trying to love each other without knowing how.

He walked a long curve of shoreline, letting the wind dry the salt on his skin. Then he spotted it — half-buried in a pocket of wet sand, a piece of driftwood bleached and knotted, twisted like it had been sculpted by something clumsy but patient.

It looked ridiculous. It looked like a chicken doing yoga. He laughed — an actual laugh, startled and short. He picked it up, brushing off the sand. He'd take it back to the lodge. Not because it was beautiful. Because it wasn't. Because it had been knocked about, shaped by tide and time, and was still here. Still solid. Like him, maybe. Like what he was becoming. Not what he had been. He tucked it under one arm and turned for home.

The sky was beginning to change again — that hour when the light softened into gold, brushing everything in a kind of hush that made it feel like the day itself was exhaling. He walked slowly, his feet finding the curve of the path through instinct more than attention, his thoughts somewhere between the weight of the past and the strange lightness that sometimes followed remembering it.

As he crested the rise near the lodge, he lifted his camera out of habit. The frame was nothing special — the angle of the grass against the dipping sun, the shadow of the fence line falling long across the sand — but his fingers moved automatically, adjusting the focus, measuring the light.

That was when he saw her.

She was further down the path, walking toward the far end of the dunes, her dog trailing behind her. Her hair was loose this time, lifted slightly by the breeze, and the low sunlight caught in the strands so that they glowed faintly. She didn't see him. Her face was turned toward the sea, not in search of anything, just... present.

He didn't lift the camera. He just watched her, unsure why. There was something about the way she moved that held him — not with grace, exactly, but with a kind of quiet certainty, like someone who belonged to this place in a way he didn't. She wasn't performing, wasn't aware of being seen, and that alone made him feel like an intruder.

He thought, briefly, of calling out. Just something small — a greeting, an apology perhaps, if he could even shape the words. But they stuck, not quite rising to the surface. Maybe it was the weight of how he'd looked at her the first time they'd met — distant, guarded, too quick to shut a door that hadn't really been opened. Maybe it was the fear of being seen when you weren't ready. Or maybe he just didn't know what he wanted to happen if she turned and looked back.

So he let her pass. She disappeared into the soft light, her figure fading into the dune path like part of the landscape. He stood for a little longer, camera hanging loosely at his side, the piece of driftwood still tucked under his arm. Then he turned slowly, walked back to the lodge, and closed the door gently behind him — not to shut the world out exactly, but to for a while with whatever that moment had stirred.

CHAPTER 8: LONDON LIGHTS.

Rafi

He woke early, and for the first time since arriving, the weight in his chest wasn't the first thing he noticed. It was still there — like something folded beneath the ribs — but lighter. Less defining. The air coming in through the open window was cool, threaded with salt and something herbal from the dunes. It moved through the room gently, like someone straightening a sheet.

He stood barefoot on the boards, drinking coffee from a chipped mug and watching the light shift across the sand. The tide was low. The day hadn't decided what it would be yet. For once, neither had he.

He picked up his phone, expecting the usual inertia, the pull of the feed. But instead, he moved methodically — deleting apps, archiving images, muting threads he no longer wanted to be part of. Instagram, gone. Twitter, gone. Photos from gallery nights, from dinners, from Saskia's last party — everything that looked polished but didn't hold anything true. It wasn't catharsis. It was quiet, practical. Like putting away clothes that no longer fit. Jules's message still hovered at the top: You alive? He smiled but didn't open it. Not yet.

Later, he walked across to the reception hut to ask about fresh towels. A simple task. Something grounded. The door stuck slightly, and he had to shove it open with his shoulder. Inside, the air was chilled and fragrant, like lemongrass candles and a memory of spa music.

Cheryl looked up from her laptop, tan glowing, white shirt pressed perfectly at the collar. Her blonde ponytail was pulled high and tight, her lashes were long, and her skin looked like it had been gently airbrushed into real life. She smiled — a slow, curated thing — and leaned slightly forward on the desk.

"Well, look who finally needs something."

"Just towels," he said, half-apologetic.

She didn't move right away. "Rafi Cyrillian," she said, tapping a long nail on the counter. "Took me a few days to place the face, but there it is. I saw your gallery show in Berlin — the light projection stuff? Stunning. And the thing with Saskia — that installation with the mirrors? Bloody genius."

He blinked, half-amused, half-exposed. "You follow art?"

"I worked in branding in London. Notting Hill for a while. Everything from influencers to hotel launches. Dated a guy who tried to build a platform called UrbanMood. Total chaos, obviously. But I learned to spot a name before it blew up." She smiled again. "You're still blowing up, by the way. Even if you're hiding out in the dunes."

He said nothing, and she handed over a folded stack of towels, her fingers brushing his hand for a fraction too long.

"This place is fine, but let's not pretend the wilderness is everything. You must miss London sometimes."

He looked at her properly then — the glossed lips, the heels that somehow didn't sink into sand, the perfect nails despite laundry duties — and for a moment, he did feel a pull. Something in her reminded him of Saskia. Not just the polish, but the performance. The practiced charisma. That high-functioning glamour that made other people want to orbit you.

"Maybe," he said. "Depends what I'm remembering."

She leaned in, like she was about to say something else — when the door burst open behind him with a gust of warm air and Ralph stepped in.

He was tall, bronzed, and wide-shouldered, all lit by that effortless surfer ease. He wore a loose tank that clung in all the right places, board shorts still damp from the sea, and his hair — bleached blond, salt-tangled — looked like it had never known a bad day. He flashed Cheryl a grin that revealed a row of perfect teeth and one dimple that could probably cause traffic accidents.

"Cheryl," he said cheerfully. "There any more of those pale ales in the back fridge? The one with the yellow label?"

Cheryl straightened, instantly perky. "You mean the craft one from Padstow? I might've hidden the last two, actually."

"For me?" He winked.

"For… someone," she said, twisting her smile.

But Ralph had already looked past her. His eyes caught on someone over Rafi's shoulder and lit up. "Hey, Iris." Rafi turned.

She was outside, stepping up from the beach, sunlit and barefoot, a rolled towel under one arm, hair tied up messily, strands escaping across her face. No makeup, no polish — just sea-flushed skin and that particular shine that came from salt and summer and not needing to try. Her dog padded alongside her, tail wagging, nose down in the sand.

"Iris," Ralph repeated, stepping out and calling lightly, "Did you get the gift I left you?"

"Yes, I will read it later - thank you," she said, smiling. "If Moss doesn't drag me into the estuary first." She kept walking, but Rafi caught it — the way her smile toward Ralph was easy, open, without hesitation.

He turned back to Cheryl, who was watching Ralph walk away with a look that was half long-suffering, half impressed. She raised an eyebrow at Rafi.

"Surfers," she said. "What they lack in humility, they make up for in abs."

Rafi didn't answer. Something inside him had tightened, subtly. Not jealousy, exactly. But a flicker of displacement. As if someone had just reminded him he didn't know the rules of this place — not like they did. Not like her.

He nodded his thanks and stepped outside, walking slowly down the boardwalk with the towels under one arm.

Halfway along the path, he heard the soft thump of paws behind him. The chocolate lab ran past again — full steam ahead, trailing sand and joy — and Iris followed, not far behind. She caught sight of him and slowed.

"He nearly took my knee out," Rafi said, looking down at the dog.

She smiled. "He's got no concept of personal space. Apologies on behalf of all Labrador-kind."

There was a pause — not awkward, but watchful.

"I wanted to say sorry," he said. "For the other day. When you brought the linen. I was…" He shook his head gently. "Sharp. Not great company."

"You were fine," she said. "Everyone has off days." Her voice was easy, and her eyes steady — not performative, not polished, just... present.

"You're from London too, right?" she asked, nodding toward the lodge.

He nodded. "I was. Not sure anymore."

"Well," she said, gesturing with her chin toward the sea, "it's a good place to be not sure in."

She turned with Moss and walked on, sand brushing off her calves as she moved. He stood for a moment longer, watching her shape blur into the brightness. She didn't look back.

Back at the lodge, he set the towels down and reached for his camera, not out of duty, but instinct. The light was slanting through the wooden slats, soft and golden, catching the edges of the driftwood on the shelf where he'd left it. He turned the lens, adjusted the focus, but didn't lift it to shoot — just looked through it, not to frame something, but to understand it.

Outside, the dune grasses bent gently in the breeze, the world moving at a pace that didn't need capturing. He let the camera settle in his lap, thinking perhaps it wasn't about what you saw, not really, but what stayed with you when you looked away.

CHAPTER 9: THE UNEXPECTED GIFT.

Iris

The book was there when she stepped outside, before the sun had properly shaken off the mist. It sat on the bench by her gate, wrapped in brown paper and tied with blue twine, her name curved across the front like a thought someone had taken time to finish.

She held it in her hands for a long moment, still barefoot, the wood cool under her soles, the sea a dull rush in the distance. Inside was a novel she'd mentioned once, in passing, after a morning surf. Ralph had been rinsing his board, hair still wet, eyes squinting against the sun, and she'd said something about books that didn't try too hard to end neatly. He'd nodded, easy and warm, like he understood the sentiment before she'd even finished the thought.

Thought you'd like this one. No grand finish. Just a good journey – Ralph.

It touched her more than she expected. Not because it was romantic — it wasn't, not really — but because it was considered. Remembered. She stood with it pressed to her chest for a breath or two, then placed it carefully on the hallway table beside the sea-glass bowl and slipped into her wetsuit before she could dwell on it.

The water was cold and restless that morning, the swell inconsistent, but the exertion helped. She paddled hard, let the waves knock the clutter from her thoughts. She told herself the flutter in her stomach had more to do with salt and wind than the memory of a note written in looping script. She didn't know Ralph. Not really. They'd exchanged a handful of words, a few glances, a shared smile under the bleached sky. And yet, something about him felt familiar. Kindred. As if someone had copied her inner weather into male form and scattered it in sand and sun.

Later that day, she'd seen him at the reception hut. He was laughing with Cheryl, leaning one hip against the counter like he belonged there. Cheryl looked as though she'd just stepped out of an interiors magazine — all pressed linen and sun-glow tan, hair in a flawless twist, gesturing with those manicured hands that always seemed to fall into the perfect shape. And then there was Rafi, standing off to the side, quiet but watching, saying little but seeing everything. Iris had hovered near the path just long enough to take it all in. Cheryl laughing lightly, leaning in. Ralph smiling, charmed. Rafi's eyes flicking from one to the other.

Cheryl was every man's idea of the finished article. The real thing. She spoke with poise, moved like she was always being filmed. She wore white and somehow never spilled. Iris, by contrast, was the chalet girl with sea-salted curls and freckles that burst into constellations at the mere suggestion of sunlight. She couldn't flirt without tripping over her own tongue. She carried sand into every room she entered.

She hadn't been trying to impress Ralph. But still. Standing there in her cut-offs and salt-washed hoodie, she'd felt like the before picture to Cheryl's after.

And Rafi. That moment between them still lingered. The apology, soft-spoken and sincere. The weight behind his eyes. A man with corners, edges. Quiet damage. And Cheryl looked ready to ease all that, smoothing him out like one of her linen shirts. Good luck to her, Iris thought. She hadn't signed up for that kind of healing.

Later, as she returned from the dunes with Moss, Ralph appeared again. They crossed paths near the low stone steps where the boardwalk gave way to grass.

"Fancy a wander up to the cliffs tomorrow?" he asked, like it was nothing, like it was natural. "I know a spot that gets the last bit of sun. I'll bring tea."

She smiled before she knew she would. "Sure. That sounds good." It did sound good. Simple. Steady. Kind.

And yet, later that night, as she folded the throw on the end of the sofa and watched the cottage lights glow one by

one across the dunes, her thoughts drifted briefly to Rafi —
his quiet apology, the faint shadow behind his eyes — she
didn't chase it. She let it float there, small and unshaped.

For now, she was walking toward something calm,
something offered gently, something that didn't ask her to
prove anything. And that, for now, felt like a beginning she
could believe in.

CHAPTER 10: CALL OF THE OCEAN.

Rafi

He woke later than usual, the filtered light brushing across the ceiling of the lodge like a thought half-formed. The silence was thick, not unpleasant, but filled with an awareness he couldn't quite shake. He lay there a while, his arm across his forehead, thinking about Cheryl.

She had leaned in close the day before, voice low, lashes flicking up like something rehearsed but still effective. She knew how to hold attention, how to draw someone into her space. She'd laughed in the exact right place, asked questions without really needing answers. It was familiar. Too familiar.

She reminded him of Saskia. Not in looks — Saskia had been angular, cool, wrapped in velvet and restraint. But in tone. The sharp, curated charm. The way she could make someone feel like the only person in the room while still cataloguing their weaknesses. Cheryl was warmer, more openly playful, but the undercurrent was the same. Rafi wasn't sure if that was comforting or cautionary.

And then there'd been Ralph. The way Cheryl lit up when he arrived, her laughter a fraction too quick, her body angling toward his without hesitation. Rafi had noticed the subtle shift, the way her gaze lingered. Ralph, of course, had taken it all in stride, grinning like it came naturally. Maybe it did. Maybe that was what people like Ralph were built for — ease, charm, balance. Rafi wasn't built that way. He knew that.

He sat up slowly, ran a hand through his hair, and stepped barefoot into the kitchen to make coffee. The kettle took longer than it should. Everything here moved in its own time, and maybe that was the point. He leaned on the counter and watched the sky through the high windows, blue pulled thin at the edges, gulls floating in lazy spirals. And then, without meaning to, his mind drifted to Iris.

The redhead with the sea-slick curls and freckles like sunbursts. He'd seen her again yesterday, at the reception hut. She'd stood just long enough to catch him watching her, before she turned away. No drama. No expression. Just... gone.

Later, he'd seen her with Ralph. Laughing. Comfortable. Like they already knew the shape of each other's silences. He'd watched them from a distance, that quiet ache curling in his chest again. Not jealousy. Just resignation.

He couldn't compete with someone like Ralph. Tall, tanned, lean-muscled, all broad shoulders and surf-weathered ease. The kind of man you saw on holiday posters, all salt spray and white smiles. Rafi was none of that. He was tall, sure, but his build was less defined, more quietly functional. His stubble grew in unevenly. He hadn't been surfing in his life.

He thought, briefly, about the only seaside trip his family had ever taken — a grey-skied afternoon in Brighton when he was eight. His parents had argued most of the day. His mum had hated the sand, complained about the wind messing up her hair. His dad had snapped about the glare on his newspaper, how he couldn't read a single line in peace. Rafi had stood at the edge of the sea, watching other children laughing in the waves, his own feet cold and bare on the pebbles. No one had gone in. They'd left after an hour, silent on the drive home.

He blinked at the memory, surprised by how clear it still was. As much as he missed them — the possibility of them, maybe — he didn't miss the tension. The forced smiles. The weight of pretending everyone was happy.

Surfing had always felt like something just out of reach. He'd wanted to try, once. Just to know what it felt like to move with the sea instead of standing stiff-legged on the shore.

Maybe he would. Maybe this would be the place. Maybe Ralph, of all people, was the one to ask. He seemed like the sort who'd laugh and offer a board without asking too many questions. Or maybe...Iris.

He thought of her, not just the wild curls or the freckles, but the way she carried herself. Quietly. No pretense. Like someone who wasn't waiting to be noticed, which made it impossible not to notice her. But she seemed caught in something already. Pulled toward Ralph's brightness, drawn to the kind of gentleness that didn't require fixing.

Maybe it was better that way. She didn't owe him anything. And he wasn't looking for anything. Not really. Still. He made a quiet promise to himself as he rinsed the coffee cup and watched the dunes shift in the breeze. He would try surfing. Even just once.

CHAPTER 11: BETWEEN THE DUNES.

Iris

She met Ralph by the two white granite posts that marked the start of the sand path, where planks edged the way down toward the beach and the coast path beyond. The morning had already begun its slow surrender to warmth, the air laced with salt and wild thyme, the sun rising above the far curve of the bay like a coin balanced on the horizon.

He greeted her with a grin and two enamel mugs tucked under one arm, a flask dangling from his fingers. "Brought the tea, as promised," he said. "Hope you don't mind mint."

She smiled. "Only if it's the real stuff." He popped the flask cap with theatrical flair and poured. It was, of course, the real stuff.

They walked together in a comfortable hush, the soft crunch of sand underfoot, Moss trailing ahead with his nose buried in tufts of sea thrift. The beach stretched out below them like a golden ribbon, three uninterrupted miles of it, curving away toward Godrevy, the lighthouse standing sentinel on the point like something from a storybook. The tide was out, revealing wide banks of firm sand patterned with the faint signatures of oystercatchers and sanderlings.

"You never get tired of this," Ralph said, gesturing out toward the sea.

Iris shook her head. "Not once. It changes every hour. Every light makes it new."

They found a patch of flattened dune grass to sit, backs to the breeze, looking out over St Ives Bay. A pair of curlews called from the estuary, their cries strange and lilting, like wind instruments on a lonely scale. She loved that sound. It reminded her that this place had always been wild, no matter how many footprints marked the shore.

Ralph poured more tea. "You ever think of leaving? Trying somewhere else?"

She shrugged. "I did, once. Thought about it. But the sea always calls me back. I think I'd be useless without it."

"That makes sense," he said. "You seem like you belong to this place. Not just in it, but of it."

His words landed softly, but deeply. She turned her face slightly, letting the wind carry the sudden heat from her cheeks. There was something so open about Ralph. Nothing hidden. What he said, he meant. There were no riddles to decode.

"What about you?" she asked. "You ever think of staying here?"

"Maybe," he said. "I like the quiet. The rhythm. There's honesty in salt and weather."

They talked for a while longer, sipping tea and letting the silence stretch without strain. He asked about her art, and she told him a little — not everything, but enough. He didn't press. He just listened, like someone who didn't need to fix anything.

At one point, his fingers brushed hers as he passed the flask. It was a small thing. Accidental, maybe. But it lingered. She caught him watching her once, his expression unreadable. Not intense. Just thoughtful. She looked away, unsure why it unsettled her.

She wanted to want this. This man beside her. This soft, sunlit morning. The view of the estuary shimmering under a sky too blue to be real. But something tugged at the edges of her calm. A shadow she couldn't name.

Ralph stood and offered her a hand. She took it, and he pulled her up easily, his fingers warm and steady around hers. They began the walk back in gentle quiet, Moss weaving circles in the sand ahead.

A curlew lifted from the grass nearby and wheeled overhead, its cry thin and wild, a single note of something ancient and unanswered. Iris tilted her face toward the sky, watching it vanish into the brightness. And for a moment, she didn't know what she was feeling. Only that it was real, and it was hers, and it was unfolding whether she wanted it to or not.

CHAPTER 12: SHORELINES

Rafi

He hadn't planned to see anyone that morning. It was supposed to be simple: a quiet walk down through the dunes, maybe catch Ralph rinsing off his board, ask a question about surfing — something light, something outward-facing. Just a small step, a brief act of bravery that wouldn't require too much of him. He told himself it didn't matter what came of it. The point was asking. Trying. Doing something instead of standing still.

The path was soft beneath his feet, dry sand mixed with crushed shells, the scent of the sea thick in the air. That quiet Cornish stillness surrounded him, broken only by the distant roll of the tide and the lazy call of gulls drifting above. The morning sun had settled into its warmest hour, gold laying low across the dunes and catching in the sharp edges of the grasses, making everything shimmer faintly like an old photograph.

And then he saw them.

It happened by accident. He'd taken the familiar turn where the planked path broke away toward the flatter stretch of sand near the estuary. He was half-thinking about how to start the conversation, how not to sound too self-conscious, when he looked up and there they were: Ralph and Iris, walking barefoot along the shoreline, hand in hand.

He froze.

They weren't saying anything, not from what he could see. But their silence wasn't empty. It was companionable, easy. The kind of quiet shared by people who had already settled into something unspoken. Iris's hair was loose and caught the wind in long ribbons, the colour like struck copper. Ralph walked beside her, body turned just enough toward hers to suggest protectiveness or maybe something more instinctual. They looked good together. They looked... right.

Rafi stood watching too long, his feet heavy, heart not broken but oddly bruised. It wasn't as if he'd expected anything. Nothing had happened between them, not really. But there had been a moment. The apology. The glance. A sense, fleeting and almost foolish, that something might shift. Now, seeing them like this, he felt that possibility close. Not with a slam, but with the quiet finality of a book set back on a shelf.

He turned away before they could notice him, his chest

tightening with something sharp and vague. He walked back the way he came, slower now, letting his hands trail through the coarse grass as if grounding himself in the movement might calm what stirred inside. The thought of surfing felt childish now, too exposed. Why had he imagined Ralph would take him seriously, that it would matter? What was he really doing here anyway? Playing at something he couldn't name. Hoping for a reset he didn't fully believe in.

By the time he reached the edge of the reception hut, his thoughts had already started shifting. If he couldn't have connection, then perhaps he could have closeness. Familiarity. Something known. And that's when Cheryl surfaced in his mind.

There had been a moment, a few days ago, when she'd laughed at something he said and touched his arm, eyes sparkling with a kind of practiced intimacy. She was glossy and confident and didn't require any guessing. Saskia would have liked her. He wasn't sure if that was a warning or a recommendation. But there was no denying the ease. She wanted to be wanted. And he, right now, wanted to stop feeling like a man constantly on the outside of something.

Not because he craved love — he didn't. Not yet. But he craved being seen. Touched. Spoken to without needing to unpick the layers first. And Cheryl, for all her sharp edges, offered something immediate. Predictable.

As he approached the hut, he caught sight of her inside, flipping through the booking folder, one leg crossed elegantly over the other, sunglasses perched in her hair. She hadn't seen him yet. He paused, hand in his pocket, rehearsing the smile he'd wear. Something light. Playful. Just enough to pass for confidence.

He wasn't proud of what he was doing. But he was tired of watching. Tired of waiting. And for one afternoon, perhaps even one hour, he wanted to feel like a man still capable of being chosen.

"Rafi!" Cheryl looked up and flashed a grin, bright and immediate. "Twice in one week. I'm honoured."

He stepped inside, casually leaning against the doorframe. "I was wondering if you knew where I could book a surfing lesson."

Her eyes widened with delighted surprise. "You? Surfing? That's something I didn't have on my bingo card. Looking for a little adrenaline?"

He shrugged, playing it down. "Thought it was time to try something new. Might as well make use of the coastline."

Cheryl uncrossed her legs slowly and set the folder aside, tilting her head as she gave him a once-over. "You don't strike me as the type to follow the crowd. You sure you want to be flopping about in a wetsuit with the rest of the holiday crowd?"

He smirked. "I thought it might be good to feel like part of the scene."

"Well," she said, voice softening, "if you really want to try something... why not something a bit more refined?"

He raised an eyebrow. "Such as?"

She stepped closer, close enough that he caught a whiff of her perfume — something sharp and expensive. "Wine tasting at Trevaskis. Sunset paddleboarding at Carbis Bay. Even pottery workshops at the old chapel in St. Erth. Something slower. More... atmospheric."

"And conveniently romantic," he said, only half teasing.

Cheryl smiled knowingly. "Well, the surf lesson board is out back if you insist, but I think you're more the slow burn type. More cove than crashing wave."

Rafi let out a low laugh, the sound surprising even him. "You always this persuasive?"

"Only when it counts," she said. "Besides, there's more than one way to let the sea in."

He didn't answer right away. Just stood there, watching her. Knowing full well what she was offering, even if she wasn't quite saying it. Knowing, too, that part of him wanted to say yes — not to the activity, but to being wanted. To letting someone reach for him first.

He nodded slowly, his voice quieter now. "Maybe I'll take a look at that pottery class."

She grinned, victorious. "Good. I'll book us two spots. You'll love it."

As he turned to leave, the air behind him warm with her perfume and implication, he felt the faintest flicker of something — not desire, not yet. But presence. It was a start.

CHAPTER 13. THE QUIET SHIFT.

Iris

Back at home, the cottage had settled into its familiar stillness. The late afternoon sun pressed long rectangles of light across the floorboards, catching on the glass jars along the windowsill, each one filled with sea-washed fragments and memories she hadn't yet named. Iris moved slowly through the kitchen, barefoot, humming something tuneless while Moss circled her feet, hopeful for crumbs.

She talked aloud to him as she chopped carrots, the way she always did when the silence pressed in too tightly. "We're a fine pair, aren't we? Me, overthinking everything. You, pretending you haven't been fed already." Moss thumped his tail against the cupboard in response.

Dinner was simple — roasted vegetables, half a loaf of bread from the bakery, a glass of red left over from the weekend.

She wasn't hungry, not really, but eating felt like a thing to do. Like anchoring herself to the evening.

Afterwards, she sat with her journal open on the table, pen in hand, but no words came. Instead, she reached for the worn leather photo album tucked beneath a basket of folded blankets. She opened it slowly, fingers trailing the edges of the old pages where photographs had begun to curl with age.

There they were. Ronald and Joyce. Her grandparents on the beach in the 1950s, squinting into the wind, thermos between them, his arm slung easily around her shoulder. Another one — him asleep in a deck chair, her grinning into the lens, freckles stark even in black and white. They had made this cottage a retreat from their farm, carved joy into its rooms with their laughter. They'd stayed in love. Not loudly, not dramatically, but in a way that had roots.

She stared at the images, wondering if that kind of love was possible anymore. If she was capable of it — or too restless, too stubborn, too fractured.

Still restless, she stood and stepped outside. The sky was bruised now, streaked with lavender and rose. The tide whispered in the distance. She thought of her rota and realised she'd never actually collected it.

The reception hut was still lit when she arrived. Cheryl was inside, leaning over the desk, phone in hand, smiling at something on the screen.

"Hey!" she called brightly as Iris stepped in. "Just finishing up. Got your rota here." She slid the paper across the desk and leaned on her elbows, eyes shining. "Big night tonight. Rafi and I are heading into town. There's a tapas pop-up at the harbour — he's got great taste, doesn't he?"

Iris forced a smile, took the paper. "Sounds fun."

Cheryl tilted her head, curious. "You okay?"

"Yeah, just tired." She tucked the rota under her arm. "Long day."

Outside, the light had dimmed further. The path felt steeper somehow. Her steps slower. Without really thinking about it, she walked to Lowen Cove. Ralph was outside, stringing up a few solar lights across the porch. He smiled when he saw her.

"Fancy a drink?" he asked. "Got some local cider chilling."

She nodded. "That sounds nice."

They sat for a while on the steps, their shoulders close, the sky dimming into the navy of early night. The conversation drifted easily, warm and unforced. Ralph had that way about him — calming, steady, the kind of man who made silence feel like comfort rather than lack. When he offered her a second glass of cider, their fingers brushed. A pause settled between them, tender and open.

"I really like being with you," he said, his voice low. "I think... I've been hoping we were heading somewhere."

Before she could answer, he leaned in and kissed her.

It was soft at first, exploratory. Then deeper, stronger — his arms enveloped her, pulling her into the warmth of his chest, the scent of salt and soap and sun lingering on his skin. Her hands rested lightly against his shoulders, her body momentarily giving in to the ease of it, the comfort. He kissed like a man who knew what it meant to be gentle.

And for a moment, she let herself feel it — the press of lips, the way his hands cupped her face, the way the world narrowed down to two heartbeats and a quiet sky.

But the noise came anyway. Doubt, uninvited, slipping in like tidewater under a door. Her mind flashed with questions, unnamed discomfort, a sudden sense of being adrift inside something that wasn't hers to hold. It was sweet, but it wasn't right. It wasn't wrong either, but it didn't settle.

She broke the kiss gently, her breath catching. "I'm sorry," she whispered, her voice barely above the sound of the sea. "You're wonderful, Ralph. But this... it doesn't feel right. It feels like... kissing my best friend."

He didn't flinch. He just nodded, eyes kind, thumb brushing a strand of hair from her cheek. "Yeah," he said softly. "I thought maybe. Just had to try."

She squeezed his hand before she stood, grateful that he made it easy to walk away without guilt. The walk back felt longer than it should have, the path winding gently beneath her feet, the air still warm with the day's last breath.

As she neared the bend between the lodges, she saw them. Rafi and Cheryl, seated close on the decking outside Lodge Eight. There was music playing — something soft, unfamiliar, lilting with brass and hush. A bottle of wine stood open between them, half-full glasses in hand. Cheryl laughed at something, tipping her head back, one hand brushing Rafi's arm.

And then Rafi looked up. Their eyes met. Just for a moment. Something stilled. He shifted, as if to rise. As if to speak. But Cheryl mistook the movement. She leaned in and kissed him.

Iris turned, quiet and invisible, her chest drawn tight. She walked the rest of the path slowly, letting the night fold around her like a blanket just shy of warm.

Back at the cottage, she dropped to the floor beside Moss and buried her face in his fur.

"Just us, mate," she whispered. "Just us tonight."

CHAPTER 14: SMOKE AND LIGHT.

Rafi

The pottery class had ended with clay beneath his fingernails and a half-shaped bowl that leaned too far to the left. Cheryl had laughed, brushing her fingers over his in a way that suggested she'd enjoyed more than the hand-building. It had been light, easy, something to keep his hands busy and his mind distracted. But it was the suggestion afterwards that changed the course of the evening.

"You have to try this pop-up place at the harbour," she said as they rinsed their hands. "Real Spanish tapas, the chef's from Valencia. I booked us a table. Hope that's alright."

He hadn't said no. Maybe he should have.

Now, hours later, he sat beneath strings of warm bulbs

stretched between old pilings, the harbour alive with music and wine and laughter that rippled like low tide through the night air. The tables were pushed together at haphazard angles, mismatched chairs filled with holidaymakers in loose linen and the golden gleam of people a little too sun-kissed and a little too wine-warm. Somewhere behind them, a busker strummed a Spanish guitar, the music soft but pulsing.

Cheryl looked radiant. Her dress skimmed her knees, pale silk that caught the breeze and clung in all the right places. Her hair was swept up, but not too neatly, and the glint of her earrings caught every flicker of candlelight. She laughed easily, too loudly perhaps, but she knew it. She liked being seen, liked the way the heads turned when she tilted her neck just so.

Rafi watched her from across the table, wine glass in hand, his skin buzzing with the slow heat of Rioja and the last of the summer sun. He wasn't drunk, but he wasn't quite sober either. He felt... suspended. Not outside himself, not lost, just floating in a version of the night he hadn't planned.

Cheryl leaned across the table, her voice lower now. "You know everyone here has been looking at us since we sat down?"

He smiled faintly. "Are they?"

"You're very photogenic, even when you're brooding." She lifted her glass. "I should know. I stalked your portfolio ages ago. London creatives couldn't get enough of you."

Rafi laughed, more breath than sound. He didn't correct her. Didn't explain how that life had worn him thin. How the images she'd seen were curated carefully over years, each one a little less like him than the last.

Cheryl's foot brushed his beneath the table. "You're thinking again. I can see it. Want to dance instead?"

He looked out at the water. The tide had rolled in quiet and steady, lapping the stone steps just beyond the string of lights. Boats bobbed gently. A couple kissed under a streetlamp, their shadows folding together like a closing book.

He turned back to Cheryl, to her wide smile and the promise of an easy night, no questions asked.

He nodded slowly. "Alright. Let's dance."

And if, for a moment, a different image flickered in his mind — red hair, the smell of salt, eyes that held something unpolished and real — he let it drift away with the tide.

CHAPTER 15: FAMILIAR STRANGERS.

Rafi

By the time they got back to Lodge Eight, the air was thick with sea mist and the kind of quiet that wraps itself around you without asking. The laughter from the harbour still rang faintly in his ears, like the echo of a party he wasn't sure he'd meant to attend. Cheryl walked ahead of him, heels in one hand, her dress clinging softly at her knees, the salt wind teasing loose tendrils of hair from her bun.

She paused on the deck and turned toward him with a soft smile, already reaching for the bottle of wine they'd brought back with them. "One more glass for the road?"

He nodded, even though his body was already beginning to

tire, the wine pooling heavily in his limbs. "Sure."

Inside, she found two mismatched tumblers in the kitchen cupboard while he lit the small outdoor lantern. The warm glow spread slowly, throwing soft shadows across the deck. Cheryl reappeared with the wine and settled beside him, folding her legs beneath her on the cushioned bench, like she belonged there.

They'd just clinked glasses when he caught movement at the edge of his vision — the slow rhythm of someone walking the path between the lodges. He turned his head just in time to see her - Iris.

She moved quietly, arms folded across her chest, a blanket draped around her shoulders. Her hair was down, catching what little light the moon offered, and Moss padded silently at her heels. She wasn't looking at them, not directly. But she saw. He knew she saw.

For a moment, he felt something hitch in his breath. He shifted slightly, about to stand, about to say something he hadn't yet formed. And then Cheryl kissed him.

It was assertive, unhesitating. She caught his jaw with one hand and pulled him to her, lips parting before his had time to meet them. Her kiss was polished, commanding — the kind of kiss that had been practiced in mirrors, perfected on other men. She tasted of Rioja and ambition, of something expensive and deeply confident. Her body leaned into his with slow control, her fingers threading into the back of his hair as if she already knew how this story was meant to go.

And for the space of that kiss — long, poised, slightly performative — he let her. Let her write him into a scene she clearly thought she was directing. But when he opened his eyes again, the path was empty. Iris was gone.

"You know," Cheryl said, pouring, "you're not at all what I expected."

"What did you expect?"

She smiled, a little too knowingly. "More ego. More performance. Less... this." She gestured around them, the quiet, the slow night, the tangle of light and shadow.

He raised an eyebrow. "Disappointed?"

"Intrigued."

They drank. The music was low now, something jazzy he'd let play from his phone, more for the atmosphere than anything else. Cheryl shifted closer, her thigh pressing lightly against his. The movement was deliberate.

"You're not over her," she said suddenly.

He looked at her, startled.

"Whoever she was," she added, with a small shrug. "I can see it in the way you hesitate. Like you're not sure what part you're playing tonight."

He didn't answer right away. Because she wasn't wrong.

He felt it — the edge of it — even as she leaned into him, her hand tracing lightly along his arm. Even as her mouth found his, soft and practiced, tasting of wine and something sweeter. He kissed her back, because it was easier than pulling away, because he wanted to feel something other than the low, persistent ache of not knowing what he wanted.

Her touch was confident, her lips warm, her laughter breathless in his ear. But somewhere in the quiet part of his mind, a different image pressed in: the sound of gulls, a girl with sea-glass freckles and wind in her hair, her eyes unreadable.

When Cheryl pulled back, her hand still resting on his chest, she tilted her head and murmured, "So... are we heading inside?"

He hesitated. Then shook his head slowly, forcing a smile that didn't quite reach his eyes. "I've got an early shoot tomorrow," he said. "Golden hour. I should probably try to get some sleep."

Cheryl pulled back just slightly, assessing. Not offended, exactly — just momentarily unreadable. Then she smiled again, all surface. "Rain check, then."

"Sure."

She rose smoothly, collected her shoes, and kissed him once more — lightly this time, a promise or a punctuation.

Rafi stayed where he was, poured the last of the wine

into his glass, and leaned back against the bench cushion, staring up at the darkening sky. The music had stopped. The phone screen dimmed. Only the hush of the waves and the occasional distant bark from a dog gave the night any rhythm.

He thought of her eyes — not Cheryl's. The other pair. Iris's. Clear, deep, unsettling. Pool blue, flecked with doubt and something that looked a lot like courage.

He drained the last sip, the wine warm on his tongue, and let the silence settle in. It was the first moment all evening that had felt real.

CHAPTER 16: SALTWATER LIGHT.

Iris

The morning came grey and pale, as if the sky hadn't quite made up its mind to begin. Iris had woken early, the air in the cottage heavy with the hush of something unresolved. Moss still lay curled at the foot of her bed, breathing slow and deep, as if even he knew there was nothing urgent about today.

She moved slowly, making tea in silence, her fingers tracing the edge of the chipped mug as the kettle whistled. The night before lingered like smoke in her chest. She hadn't dreamt it — she knew that. She'd seen them. Cheryl's laughter like glass in the dark, the slow lean-in, the kiss. Rafi not resisting. It wasn't even the kiss that had stung. It was the ease of it. The way it had slotted into place like it had happened before and would happen again. It hadn't broken her. But it had shifted something.

She left the mug half-full on the counter and pulled on her wetsuit, the motion familiar, grounding. Her body moved through the rhythm of it without question, like muscle memory stitched into her bones. She grabbed her board and whistled for Moss, who padded sleepily to the door and flopped down just outside it, content to wait.

The air was cold as she stepped out, the kind of cold that bites but doesn't bruise. Fog hovered low over the dunes, muffling sound and distance. The sand was damp and dark, studded with old shells and tangled fronds of seaweed. She made her way to the beach, board under one arm, breath visible in the sharp morning light. The sea was silver. No one else out yet. Perfect.

She waded in quickly, the water slicing clean lines against her skin, shocking and necessary. Her board bobbed beside her, eager. As she paddled out beyond the first break, the rhythm settled into her bones. The water, the sky, her breath — all aligned. All honest. All hers.

She didn't think about them. Not consciously. But with every wave, every glide, every fall and rise, she felt something loosening. Not forgiveness, maybe. But distance. Space for air. For clarity.

After her surf, she showered quickly at the beach tap and dressed into soft layers, stuffing her board back behind the cottage. Then came the usual rhythm of her day: towels to collect from two of the Towans lodges, sand to sweep, welcome baskets to refresh. Her hands moved quickly and efficiently. The routine was comfort, its predictability soothing. Every lodge had its quirks — a sliding door that stuck, a wonky lamp, the driftwood mirror that refused to stay straight — but it was hers to tend to, and she liked that. Cheryl wasn't around when she popped into reception. That was a small mercy.

By late morning, Iris was walking the long estuary path into Hayle, Moss trotting ahead, tail swishing, the sky still bright and mild. Boats bobbed on the water, and the smell of wet salt and distant pastries carried on the breeze. Her parents' house sat on a quiet road near the estuary, white-walled with a low stone fence, and the garden spilling with colour in its usual, slightly unkempt charm. Flowers crowded the front wall in soft explosions of purple and yellow. Her mum opened the door before she even knocked.

"I saw you coming," Frances said, already pulling her into a hug. "You alright, love?"

They sat at the kitchen table, mugs of strong tea between them, Moss curled on the mat. The kitchen hadn't changed in years — lace at the windows, worn pine table, the calendar with hand-written reminders looping around the corners. Her dad was out helping her brother Tom on a build near St Erth. It was quiet in that comforting way only family homes can be.

Iris found herself talking more than she meant to. About Ralph. About the kiss that hadn't felt like a kiss should. About the man in Lodge Eight who unsettled her without trying to. She said his name this time — Rafi — and her mother didn't ask questions, just listened. Frances poured more tea and wrapped her hands around her own mug like she was warming something fragile.

"You don't have to know what it is yet," she said, gently. "Just be careful not to mistake intensity for connection. They're not the same thing."

"I keep thinking I should stop hoping for something big. Something lasting. Maybe I've built it up too much."

Her mum smiled, a little sadly. "Your grandparents were lucky. What they had — that kind of steady love — it's rare. Not everyone finds it. But that doesn't mean what you find won't matter. Even the ones that don't last."

They talked a while longer, about safer things — Tom's daughters, the new bakery in Lelant, the mischief Moss got up to. But when Iris hugged her before she left, she held on a little longer than usual, grateful and aching in equal measure.

Back home, she let Moss nap while she returned to her workspace. The painting from the morning was still wet, colour bleeding at the edges. She added more to it without thinking — deeper blues, sharper whites. Movement. The brush felt easier in her hand than it had in days. She wasn't looking for meaning. Only for something that felt like truth.

Later, as the light shifted and the sky began its slow slide into evening, she picked up a piece of green sea glass from the sill and held it to the window. She turned it between her fingers, watching the light flicker through its soft edges, through the fogged green made beautiful by time and weather and abrasion.

"Whole," she murmured. "Despite the breaking."

It wasn't a promise. Just a reminder. Outside, the tide turned.

CHAPTER 17: THE MORNING AFTER.

Rafi

The light crept in slowly, slipping across the bare wooden floorboards and onto the edge of the bed where Rafi sat upright, already dressed. He hadn't really slept. Not properly. The wine had left his mouth dry, and his limbs heavy, and though the air in the lodge was still, it pressed in on him with quiet accusation.

He made coffee without thinking, the motions automatic, comfort through repetition. The silence clung, stretching itself thin around the remnants of Cheryl's perfume and laughter. She'd left quickly last night, from the decking, her laughter fading into the dusk as she descended the steps, heels swinging from one hand, her exit light and unbothered. He had offered a lie without hesitation — a shoot at golden hour. An early start. She had smiled knowingly, as though she'd expected as much all along.

Now, the mug was warm in his hands, but the taste was flat. He stood at the kitchen counter, looking out toward the dune line, fog still nestled low across the horizon. A gull wheeled above, its cry thin and aimless. He should photograph something.

He hadn't picked up his camera in three days, not properly. The last shots had felt hollow, staged. But today, something in his chest tugged. Not guilt exactly. Not longing. Something quieter. A need to reconnect.

He slung the camera strap across his shoulder and stepped out into the morning. The sand was cool beneath his feet as he made his way along the boardwalk and down onto the beach. Light was lifting now, stretching pale gold across the tide line. He adjusted his lens, took a few test shots of nothing in particular — broken shells, long shadows of dune grass, the ripple of a dog's paw print. And then, through the mist, a figure appeared.

A surfer, just beyond the break. Moving with rhythm, cutting through the water, shoulders strong and silhouette certain. He raised the camera instinctively, focus tightening. Iris. Her red hair, wet and darkened, was slicked back beneath a simple neoprene hood. She paddled effortlessly, then turned, caught a wave, and rode it all the way to the shallows with easy grace.

He lowered the camera. Then raised it again. It felt wrong. Intrusive. But he didn't stop. He adjusted the lens, the shutter whispering open and closed, catching light and movement and something else he hadn't planned to see.

She hadn't noticed him. Or maybe she had and was pretending not to. He didn't know which hurt more. As she pulled her board out of the surf, Moss bounded up from the shoreline, circling her with tail-wagging enthusiasm. She scratched behind his ears, laughing softly, the sound lost to him but visible in her mouth, in the way her shoulders relaxed.

He stepped back, let the camera fall to his chest. His breath fogged in front of him. The images flashed on the screen, one by one. She looked alive in them. Uncurated.Whole.

He blinked, and for a moment the images blurred with another memory. London. The night everything stopped.

It had been loud. A rooftop party. The clink of glasses, the buzz of clients, Saskia in that red dress with a neckline sharp as her voice. A fight. No, not a fight — a reckoning. Words that couldn't be taken back. Words said about him, not to him. About what he had become. About what he was failing to be.

And the next morning, the headlines. A photograph not taken by him but of him — used without permission, circulated, dissected. He'd hated the way his own face looked in it. Blank. Caught. He'd booked the train that afternoon. And never looked back.

Now, standing on the sand, the tide inching closer to his boots, he lifted his camera one more time. But this time, he didn't shoot. He watched Iris walk back up toward the dunes, Moss at her side, the board balanced under her arm. Then he turned, and walked in the opposite direction.

CHAPTER 18: SOMETHING ELSE ENTIRELY.

Rafi

She turned up mid-morning, wearing oversized sunglasses and carrying a pastry box from the bakery in Lelant as if she'd done it a hundred times before. Rafi had only just returned from the dunes, salt still on his skin, the camera cooling in his hands. He hadn't planned on seeing anyone. Certainly not her.

"Thought I'd brighten your day," Cheryl said breezily, holding out the box. "Hazelnut pain au chocolat. Still warm. You're welcome."

He hesitated, then took it with a nod. "Thanks."

She let herself onto the decking without waiting for an

invitation, plopping down into the cushioned seat with the air of someone claiming her space. "You disappeared on me last night. Not that I didn't expect it, Mr Golden Hour."

Rafi forced a half-smile, setting the pastry aside. "Early light waits for no one."

Cheryl pulled out a folded newspaper from her bag. It was this week's edition of the lifestyle magazine he used to freelance for. She unfolded it and spread it across her knees with theatrical care.

"Still on the cover," she said, tapping the image. One of his shots. A double-page spread. A woman in monochrome against steel and glass. Cold, perfect, detached.

He looked at it and felt nothing.

"You know," she added, leaning forward, "you could still be doing this. We could be doing this. Imagine what people would say if you brought me back to London. You, reformed. Me, radiant. Honestly, Rafi, this place—" she gestured to the dunes beyond the lodge "—it's charming, sure, but come on. You're not really planning to rot in some Cornish tourist trap while the city forgets you, are you?"

He didn't answer straight away.

She laughed lightly, misreading the pause. "Unless... is this about her? You're still brooding over Saskia, aren't you? Look, I know she messed with your head, but you can't hide in sand dunes forever."

Rafi stood, pacing to the edge of the deck. The breeze was rising now, catching the corners of the magazine still on her lap.

"I'm not hiding," he said, quietly.

"Then what are you doing?" she asked, her voice softening but still edged with amusement. "Because it looks a lot like avoidance."

He turned. "I'm trying to figure out who I am without being seen through someone else's lens."

Cheryl tilted her head, lips parting as if to argue, but the words didn't come. After a beat, she stood too, brushing crumbs from her jeans.

"Okay," she said, tone shifting. "Well. That was dramatic. Maybe I caught you on the wrong day."

She kissed his cheek, lingered just a moment too long, and then walked away, her perfume trailing in the warm air.

When she was gone, Rafi stepped back inside and sat at his laptop. The photos were still open from earlier. He clicked through them one by one: sea, foam, board, the graceful figure in the water.

Iris.

He began adjusting the light. Not for drama. For truth. He didn't know why he was doing it. Only that he had to. And as the image sharpened under his hand, something inside him did too.

CHAPTER 19: THE CLICK OF THE SHUTTER.

Iris

Iris had intended to slip in and out quickly. Just drop off the fresh linen, fluff the cushions, check the water pressure, and go. Lodge Eight was first on her list that morning, and she'd deliberately set off early, hoping to avoid any awkward encounters. But life never quite worked the way you wanted when you most needed it to.

She pushed open the lodge door with her hip, balancing the linen bag on one shoulder. Moss stayed on the porch, instinctively sensing her mood. Inside, the air was still. Cool. She moved quietly through the open-plan space, folding towels with mechanical precision, smoothing the corners of the bed like it mattered.

He was there. Of course he was. At the far end of the lodge, Rafi sat at his laptop, headphones on, fingers moving in short, purposeful gestures across the trackpad. He hadn't noticed her.

She considered slipping back out. But then he looked up. Their eyes met. A beat passed. He pulled the headphones down, offering a cautious, polite smile. "Morning."

She forced a smile in return. "Didn't mean to interrupt. Just dropping these off."

"You're not interrupting."

She lingered near the kitchen counter, fingers twitching against the smooth granite. The awkwardness clung to the walls.

"You working on something new?" she asked lightly, gesturing toward his laptop. Small talk. Safe ground.

He hesitated. Then nodded. "Sorting through yesterday's shoot. The light was... something else."

She nodded, unsure why she hadn't already walked out.

Then he added, too casually, "I took some shots of the water yesterday morning. Caught a surfer just as the light came in over the dunes."

She stilled.

His eyes flicked up to meet hers. "It was you. I didn't realise at first. You were... you looked..."

"You took pictures of me?" she asked, her voice sharper than she intended.

Rafi straightened slightly. "I know I should have asked. I'm sorry. It was instinct more than anything. I wasn't trying to... I mean, it wasn't about you, exactly. The moment was just... beautiful. The movement. The colour. It felt honest."

She didn't reply right away. A flush was rising to her cheeks. Not quite embarrassment. Not quite anger.

"You could have asked."

"I know. You're right."

Silence stretched between them. Her fingers clenched slightly around the edge of the linen bag. And yet, somewhere under the annoyance was something else. A flicker of something she didn't want to name. The idea that someone had seen her without her knowing. That she had been worth capturing.

She looked at him again. Really looked. The uncertainty in his eyes. The apology, unguarded.

"Can I see them?" she asked, her voice quieter now.

He blinked. "Of course."

He turned the laptop toward her, scrolling slowly through

the images. Wave after wave, light breaking, seafoam catching in arcs. And there she was. Small in the frame. Then closer. Balanced, focused, her hair slicked back, eyes on the horizon. She didn't speak. The silence was reverent now.

When she finally looked up, something in her had shifted.

"You have a good eye," she said.

He smiled. Softly. "Only when the light's right."

She turned back toward the door, the linen now forgotten on the counter. Moss stirred.

"Thanks," she said. "For showing me."

He didn't say anything as she left. But the click of the shutter still echoed long after she was gone.

CHAPTER 20: A LITTLE OFF CENTRE.

Iris

Iris tried to focus. She had a checklist in her back pocket, her usual rota scribbled in her own loopy handwriting, the paper soft at the corners from weeks of folding and unfolding. The breeze that drifted between the lodges was balmy, carrying the scent of salt and sun-warmed grass, and the occasional waft of someone's overambitious barbecue. Somewhere, gulls called to each other over the dunes. It should have been the kind of morning she slipped into easily — but today, her head was elsewhere.

Somewhere between Lodge Two and the bin store behind Lodge Nine, she'd lost track of what she was doing. She'd replaced a welcome basket with two bags of dog food. Left tea bags in a shower caddy. Fluffed a pillow with the TV remote still inside it. When she caught herself about to wipe down the window ledge with hand lotion instead of polish, she groaned aloud. Even Moss gave her a sidelong glance of quiet disapproval, trotting faithfully behind her but with a noticeable wag of amused disbelief.

"Don't start," she muttered, glancing back at him with a rueful smile. "I know. I'm off my game."

But how could she concentrate when Rafi's face kept swimming back into her thoughts? Those eyes. Intent, apologetic. The way he'd looked up at her, equal parts guilt and something softer, something almost reverent.

She'd been cross at first, caught off guard, but the feeling had softened with distance. Now it hovered in her mind, like the aftertaste of a dream you didn't want to wake from. Not unpleasant. Just... distracting.

She could still see his hands on the laptop, scrolling through the photos slowly, like each one mattered. Like she mattered. And the way he hadn't tried to charm his way out of it or deflect with some urbane excuse. He'd just told the truth. That it hadn't been about her at first. But then it had become something else. Her.

She nearly doused her own foot in lemon cleaner, caught herself just in time, and gave a startled laugh that startled a nearby jackdaw into flight.

"Brilliant, Iris. Truly professional," she muttered, shaking her head and moving on.

By early afternoon, the jobs were done — or at least close enough for a workday. The lodges were swept and straightened, the bins discreetly tucked back behind their screens, the welcome biscuits replenished and aligned with quiet pride.

Back at the cottage, the quiet felt expansive. She peeled off her sandy trainers, washed her hands under cold running water, and tied her damp hair into a knot at the crown of her head. Her old sweatshirt, paint-splattered and soft with age, went over her shoulders like armour. The easel stood in its usual place near the wide front window, bathed in the waning light of the day, and the half-finished painting from the night before seemed to glow with invitation.

This time, she didn't hesitate.

The brush felt good in her hand — familiar and sure. She worked quickly, letting instinct take the lead, smoothing soft creams into the sky, dragging deeper blues into the suggestion of shadowed dunes. Sea-glass greens curled along the edges of the surf, the lines fluid and bold. Her thumb smudged highlights with the same casual affection she might use to brush sand from Moss's ear. Her chest ached with it — not sadness, exactly, but the fullness of something real taking shape.

By the time she stepped back, the light in the room had changed. Her tea had gone cold beside the sink. Moss was curled up in the corner, snoring softly, paws twitching in some sun-drenched dream.

And she was proud. Really proud.

The piece wasn't polished or perfect. But it was hers. No

mimicry. No overthinking. Just her eye, her hand, her moment.

She slipped outside to the shed and rummaged through the box of old driftwood frames, fingers brushing over weathered edges until one clicked into place. It was imperfect — warped at one side, knotted with salt — but it fit. She cleaned the glass carefully, sealed the back, and lifted it in both hands. For a long while, she just stood there, cradling the finished piece like it might shift if she breathed too hard.

She hung it beside the photo of her grandparents. Ronald, grinning into the wind, his cap askew; Joyce, scarf knotted at her throat, eyes almost closed against the sun. The two of them captured in that way only love makes possible.

"There," Iris whispered.

And for the first time in a long while, she didn't feel like she was pretending.

Something had shifted. Quietly. Completely.

CHAPTER 21: CRACKS IN THE SILENCE.

Iris

It started with the sound of tyres crunching on the gravel outside the cottage. Iris glanced up from the dish she was rinsing, the light still warm across the kitchen floor, and spotted a familiar white van parked awkwardly halfway between the gate and the rosemary bush she'd been meaning to trim back for weeks.

The side door slid open with a screech, and out tumbled three familiar figures, squealing with delight. Mae led the charge, tall for her age and already mid-sentence about something she'd seen in the dunes, while her older sisters Molly and Elsie followed close behind, all knotted hair and sun-pinked cheeks.

"Auntie Iris!" shouted Molly, her plaits already coming

undone.

Tom followed a beat later, looking dishevelled in the way only a man juggling three energetic daughters and an overloaded tool bag could. His t-shirt was streaked with something that looked suspiciously like poster paint, and one of his shoelaces was undone. "Hope you don't mind the ambush," he said, lifting a brow. "Mum mentioned you had a quiet afternoon."

"Mum always has a loose grip on the definition of 'quiet'," Iris replied, already laughing as she opened the door wider to let them all barrel inside.

The kids swarmed through the cottage like sunbeams, dragging in sand and questions and half-finished anecdotes. Moss was in heaven. Iris set out squash and biscuits while Tom collapsed into one of the mismatched chairs and rubbed a hand across his face.

"You alright?" she asked gently.

"Yeah. Work's been chaos. Building out toward Connor Downs now, and half the site got held up by missing timber. Needed a break. Thought we'd bring the chaos to you."

She handed him a biscuit. "Much appreciated."

They chatted as the children pulled colouring books from the cupboard and began loudly negotiating crayon territory. At one point, Tom wandered over to the wall beside the fireplace and paused in front of the new painting. His brow furrowed in appreciation as he stepped closer.

"Iris," he said, softly. "This is brilliant. I mean it. The colour, the texture... is that sea glass?"

She glanced up from pouring juice. "A few pieces. It felt right."

"It more than feels right. The way it catches the light in the corner... and this frame—the driftwood? It's inspired. You always did have an eye, but this is... it's something else."

She shrugged lightly, brushing off the praise. "Just something I threw together." But her cheeks warmed, and she turned her back to him a little too quickly.

"Come on," he said, grinning. "You know it's good. I'm proud of you."

She didn't say anything for a moment. Just smiled into the jug of squash, heart softening. Tom always got her. Always had. It was comforting, grounding. Tom had always been her anchor. And sometimes, without saying much, he just knew when she needed him.

After a lull, he looked at her with a quiet curiosity. "So... the guy from Lodge Eight. What's his story?"

Iris didn't meet his gaze right away. "What do you mean?"

"You tell me. You've looked like someone's turned your world sideways this week. Mum said you were distracted. That's rare."

She picked at the edge of a coaster. "There's nothing going on. He's just... not what I expected."

"That sounds exactly like something going on."

She gave a half-smile, unsure how to explain Rafi without explaining too much. "He's complicated."

"Aren't we all?"

They left it there. That was the thing with Tom. He knew when not to push.

Later, after they'd packed up the biscuit crumbs and rescued half-melted crayons from beneath the radiator, she walked them to the van. Elsie fell asleep almost instantly, her cheek smushed against Mae's shoulder in the back seat.

Tom wrapped her in a brief, tight hug. "Don't overthink it, Sis. Just... let something be good for a change."

She watched the van disappear down the lane, the sound of it fading into the hush of early evening.

Back inside, the cottage felt strangely quiet, the kind of silence that reveals what it was holding back. She sat on the floor next to Moss and ran a hand through his ears, watching the shifting shadows across the walls.

She thought of Rafi. The way he'd looked at her when she asked to see the photos. Like she was something worth showing. Worth keeping. Maybe that was the problem. She wasn't used to being seen that way. Not by someone like him. And she wasn't sure what it meant yet. But for the first time, she wanted to find out.

CHAPTER 22: ASK ME ANYTHING.

Rafi

The light was strange that morning. Not dramatic, not gold-drenched or broken through with shafts of brilliance. It was quiet light—the sort that settled on the skin without announcing itself. Rafi wandered the edge of the dunes with his camera in hand, the strap looped loosely around his wrist, though he hadn't lifted it once.

He told himself he was looking for something specific: a certain curve of the bay, the way the mist clung to the marram grass, the hint of tide creeping in with soft persistence. But really, he was just avoiding the images on his laptop, the ones that felt too close and too far all at once. Avoiding the unread message from Cheryl. Avoiding the version of himself she still expected him to be.

He no longer wanted that world—the curated sharpness of it, the endless performance, the constant need to impress or brand or please. He had lived it long enough to know what it cost. But here, in this stripped-back space between dunes and sea, he wasn't yet sure what he wanted instead.

It was the in-between that unnerved him. The ambiguity. The space where something new might begin, but nothing had settled yet. Then he saw her. Iris.

She was crouched near a low bank of sea-pink, her hair pulled back loosely, a bucket beside her and a piece of driftwood in her hands. Moss lay nearby, eyes half-closed, ears flicking every so often in the direction of distant birdsong. There was a peace to her posture, something entirely unforced, as though she belonged to the landscape rather than simply moving through it.

He froze. She hadn't seen him. He could turn around. But something in the way she brushed the hair from her face, the soft concentration in her brow, made him stay rooted. He took a breath and walked down the slope.

She looked up as he approached, her expression guarded but not closed. "You alright?"

"Yeah," he said. "Just... walking."

She nodded toward the camera. "With your camera?"

"Habit," he replied, then paused. "And maybe hoping to see something worth stopping for."

She tilted her head slightly but didn't speak. He shifted his weight, the sand shifting underfoot. "Actually, I was wondering if I could ask you something."

That caught her interest. "Go on, then."

He rubbed the back of his neck, the words slower now, careful. "Would you show me the coast? The real version of it. Not the tourist brochure shots, not the polished paths. The places that matter. To you."

Iris blinked, clearly surprised. Her lips parted like she was about to ask why, but instead she said, "Why me?"

He hesitated. Then said, truthfully, "Because you see it differently. You don't look at this place like it's a view. You look at it like it's alive. I've spent years taking pictures of things I didn't really understand. I don't want to do that anymore."

She looked past him then, toward the curve of the bay, her eyes catching the shimmer off the sea like they belonged to it. For a long moment, the silence stretched between them—not uncomfortable, but weighted.

Finally, she spoke. "Alright."

He blinked. "Really?"

"Not all in one go. And I'm not carrying your tripod."

A laugh escaped him, light and honest. "Deal."

They walked together, not talking much at first. Just the shuffle of boots in soft sand, the distant call of terns, the sea humming in the background like a steady breath.

He didn't lift the camera once. And for the first time in a long while, he didn't feel like he needed to.

CHAPTER 23: SCRATCHING THE SURFACE.

Rafi

They set off just after lunch, Iris climbing into the passenger side of Rafi's ageing Land Rover with the kind of ease that made it look like she'd driven one herself once upon a time. Moss took up his usual position in the back, tongue lolling, tail thudding softly against the wheel well. The windows were down, sea air spilling in, and the radio flickered between static and the faint hum of some 90s indie track Rafi hadn't heard in years.

Their first stop was Gwithian Beach. Iris led the way down a path fringed with soft grasses and bursts of thrift, her pace unhurried but purposeful. The sand was wide and golden, stretching far ahead under a pale blue sky. Water lapped at the shore in slow, clean curls, and a few early surfers bobbed out in the break, waiting for something worth riding. Rafi watched them for a long moment before lifting his camera. This time, he asked. Iris just nodded.

They wandered the beach, barefoot now, the tide tugging playfully at their ankles. Iris showed him the rock pools she used to hunt for crabs in as a girl, pointed out a cove where seals sometimes slipped in to sleep during storms. Her voice was easy here, her laugh looser.

They ate late lunch at a small cliffside café, perched above the shoreline. She ordered something with fresh crab; he chose a pasty the size of his forearm and ate it like a man who'd earned it. Conversation wandered. She told him about the time she'd tried to swim across the estuary as a teenager and had to be towed back by an amused lifeguard. He shared a story about a disastrous fashion shoot in Soho that ended with a model storming off in a dress worth more than his old apartment.

From there, they drove to Mutton Cove, where the seals sprawled like sun-struck mermaids across black rock. Rafi crouched to get the angle just right, but ended up watching more than shooting. Their heavy, lazy stillness reminded him of something he hadn't felt in a long time. The opposite of urgency. A lesson in stillness.

The final stop was the King George V Memorial Walk, a path that wound gently along the edge of the estuary, flanked by exotic plants and old stone benches. Iris spoke less now, letting the sounds of birds and the ripple of water fill the space. Rafi was grateful. The ache in his legs was catching up with him—his city self not quite accustomed to this kind of movement. But he didn't say anything.

The walk ended at the edge of the outdoor swimming pool, a still stretch of turquoise behind a low fence. The light was softer now, late afternoon slipping into evening, and the air had taken on a chill.

He stood there, hands resting on the top of the fence, breath catching slightly.

"You alright?" Iris asked, watching him.

"Yeah," he said. "Just tired. I think my lungs forgot what fresh air felt like."

She smiled, a flicker of amusement in her eyes. "And this is only the start. You've barely scratched the surface."

He turned toward her then, genuinely, and nodded.

"I hope we keep going."

She didn't answer. But she didn't look away, either.

Later, as they approached the Land Rover together in the soft blue hush of evening, Rafi felt something in him settle. Not in the way things settled when they were finished, but like dust finally touching ground after being suspended in the air too long. He glanced at Iris beside him—her hair lifted slightly by the breeze, her expression calm, unguarded—and thought of how rare it was to be near someone who didn't perform for the world.

She hadn't tried to impress him. She hadn't flattered or flirted or filled the silences with noise. And still, she'd left him full. She carried the place inside her, that was clear, but more than that—she carried a kind of truth. And for the first time in months, maybe longer, he didn't feel like running from what he felt.

CHAPTER 24: THE DRIVE BACK.

Iris

They were quiet on the drive back. Not uncomfortable silence, but the kind that settled between two people who no longer needed to fill every moment. The sun had begun to slip behind a soft haze of cloud, turning the sky a muted peach, and the sea glimmered out on the horizon, calm and knowing.

Iris leaned against the window, her cheek cooled by the glass, the familiar rattle of Rafi's Land Rover oddly soothing. Her limbs ached pleasantly from the walking, the sea air still clinging to her skin. It had been a good day—unexpectedly good. Rafi had surprised her. Not just with his willingness to see, but his effort to listen. To really be present.

They turned off the coast road and began the gentle climb

toward the Towans, the tyres bumping over the uneven gravel path that snaked up to the lodges. Iris sat up a little straighter, mind already drifting to the checklist she'd left half-finished that morning—towels to fold, bins to check.

But then she saw them. Cheryl, emerging from the front door of Lowen Cove with her unmistakable strut, her usually polished blonde hair slightly dishevelled, the collar of her linen shirt misaligned, and something in her step just a little too self-satisfied. Behind her, Ralph appeared shirtless in the doorway, laughing at something she said and running a hand through his sun-bleached hair. He leaned casually against the frame, clearly at ease.

The implications hung in the air like low cloud. They didn't need to hear what was said. It was written in the curve of Cheryl's smile, in the way she adjusted her shirt with one hand and tossed her hair back like it had been well-used.

Beside her, Rafi went still. His hands tightened around the steering wheel, jaw clenching almost imperceptibly. He didn't speak.

And Iris... she folded into herself.

Of course. Cheryl, even rumpled, looked like she belonged on the cover of a magazine. The kind of woman men fell over themselves for. Of course Rafi had noticed. Maybe he still wanted her. Maybe he never stopped.

How could Iris compare to that? With her tangled hair, freckled skin, her life of linen changes and sand-filled dog bowls. Cheryl was polish and presence. Iris was... utility.

Familiar. Ordinary.

Iris felt the air in the Land Rover shift, her lungs tightening around something she couldn't quite name. Not hurt. Not jealousy, not exactly. Just a sort of jolt. A misstep. The sharpness of seeing something that confirmed what you hadn't wanted to think about.

Rafi didn't seem to notice. Or if he did, he said nothing. His gaze stayed forward, hands steady on the wheel.

Iris turned her face back toward the window.

"Everything alright?" he asked, glancing over.

"Yeah," she said, too quickly. Then softened it. "Just tired."

He nodded. "Me too."

They pulled up outside her cottage. Rafi kept his eyes on the windscreen, his grip on the steering wheel still firm, knuckles pale beneath the skin. He stared straight ahead, jaw tight, saying nothing for a long beat.

"Thanks for the day," he said at last, his voice flat, formal, as though they were strangers parting ways after a polite meeting.

Iris reached for the door handle, pausing. "Sure," she said, her own voice quieter now.

He didn't move to help her down. Didn't offer the open warmth of before. Just nodded once, eyes never leaving the horizon.

She stepped out onto the gravel, clicked for Moss to follow, the door closing behind her with a muted click.

Rafi shifted the gearstick and pulled away without another glance.

"We might," she said.

Then she turned toward the cottage, the door swinging shut behind her with a quiet finality she didn't quite feel.

Iris stood for a moment just inside the door, hand still resting on the handle. Something tightened in her chest, low and unspoken. She couldn't stop thinking about Ralph. How long had it been going on with Cheryl?

The book he'd left her, the soft glances, the easy charm—it had all felt genuine. But now, it seemed like something she'd misread entirely. She felt duped, but mostly unsettled. She had let herself believe in the possibility of something simple, something kind. And now it felt like it had been part performance, part comfort.

But it wasn't Ralph and Cheryl that stayed with her—it was Rafi's reaction. The way he had gripped the wheel, gone rigid beside her. Like something had hit him just as hard. That, more than anything, rattled her. If he didn't care, he'd have looked away. He'd have joked or smirked. But he hadn't.

Still, it didn't matter. Not really. Rafi and Cheryl made

sense. Beautiful, polished people who knew how to move in the world. She couldn't compete with that. She wasn't even sure she wanted to. But the thought of it still stung. Not hurt. Not jealousy, not exactly. Just a kind of quiet undoing. The unravelling of a thread she hadn't realised she was holding so tightly.

She'd been foolish. This wasn't something. Not to him. Not when there were women like Cheryl still in the picture.

Let them have her, Iris thought. They clearly both wanted her—Rafi and Ralph—each dancing around whatever attraction or history or impulse had driven them to her doorstep. She wasn't going to be the afterthought, the one they came to once the glitter wore off. If Cheryl was the main event, let her be. She refused to be the consolation prize, the quiet fallback when the drama ran dry. She wouldn't let herself get tangled in someone else's triangle—or square, or whatever this ridiculous shape had become.

CHAPTER 25: BRUISED EDGES.

Rafi

He drove without music. The Land Rover rattled and hummed over the gravel path, but inside the cab, the silence was heavy. Not the kind he liked—the kind filled with birdsong and sea air, where the world hushed around a lens. This was the other kind. The silence of something lost before it had found its footing.

He gripped the wheel tighter than he needed to, jaw clenched until it ached. Cheryl and Ralph. It had been like walking into a scene he hadn't meant to witness, the sort of moment that should have faded behind a closed door. But there it was, right in front of them—messy hair, easy grins, a shirt hastily buttoned. And Iris had seen it all, too.

Her silence afterward had said everything.

Rafi replayed her expression again and again. The way her

posture changed, folding in, drawing back. And yet when he glanced over, when he asked if she was alright, her eyes weren't on Cheryl. They were on Ralph. That was what gutted him the most.

She still cared. For Ralph. The way her shoulders dipped, not in outrage but something closer to defeat. He'd recognised it. That kind of ache. That particular brand of realisation. He'd felt it before—when Saskia stopped pretending she wasn't already gone.

He had no right to feel it now. But the sting was there. Sharp. Unwelcome.

Iris hadn't looked at him the way she had looked at Ralph, not even during the beach walk or over coffee in that cliffside cafe. And why would she? Ralph was built for this place—sunkissed, at ease in salt and sun, a man whose smile didn't need translation. Rafi felt like a mistake in hiking boots, always arriving half a beat behind.

Still, something in her silence had unsettled him. She hadn't said goodbye the same way. No warm nod. No quiet thanks. He'd tried to play it cool. Not to let the crack show. But he knew he'd sounded clipped. Distant. He hadn't meant to. Or maybe he had.

He hated how familiar it all felt. Cheryl and Ralph, so visibly pleased with themselves, as if the world bent naturally toward their confidence. It wasn't jealousy exactly—at least not of Ralph—but more a bitter echo of something that still lived inside him. Saskia had been like that too. Poised, admired, sharp at the edges. She could claim a room with a glance, and for a long time, Rafi had thought proximity to that kind of brilliance made him brighter too. But it hadn't. It had burned him out.

Watching Cheryl toss her hair like it was all a game, watching Ralph grin with that surf-drenched ease—it brought it all back. The illusion. The slow, creeping realisation that he'd been orbiting someone who never really saw him.

And now Iris. Still quiet, still watching Ralph with eyes he didn't want her to have. If there was pain in her silence, he couldn't tell who it belonged to. That's what got under his skin. Not knowing. Not being able to ask.

He parked the Land Rover outside his own lodge and sat there for a long while, engine off, staring out at the line of dunes beyond. He needed to stop thinking about her. But he didn't get out. Not yet.

CHAPTER 26: LINEN AND THORNS.

Iris

The staff meeting was meant to be quick. Just a changeover check-in, a quick chat about supplies and guest notes, a rota review. But Cheryl had turned up glowing—sunned, smug, and practically radiating satisfaction. Iris barely recognised her. Her usual crisp shirt was swapped for something softer, looser, with the faintest shimmer of yesterday still in her hair.

Everyone noticed. No one said it. But they noticed. Cheryl breezed into the Dune Lodges reception, clipboard in hand, coffee she hadn't made herself steaming beside her. "Busy weekend ahead," she said, too brightly. "I hope you've all had your Weetabix."

Iris stood beside the wall-mounted calendar pretending to study linen counts, but her shoulders prickled. The other staff exchanged polite smiles, nodding in the way you did when someone had clearly had a better night than you.

Cheryl perched herself on the edge of the reception desk like a talk show host. "Between us girls," she said, lowering her voice in a stage whisper, "is it just me or is summer looking promising? A brooding photographer with a broken heart, or a muscular surfer with abs to die for? Honestly, I don't know where to start."

There were titters around the room. Iris didn't join in. Her throat felt tight, her clipboard suddenly very interesting. She didn't look up. Couldn't. She didn't want to know. And yet, she did.

Cheryl turned toward her then, smile sharp. "And you, Iris. Who was that dishy bloke who came to see you last week? With the kids? Tall. Stubbled. Handsome. I nearly offered him a complimentary stay."

Iris blinked. "That was my brother, Tom."

Cheryl's face faltered for half a second, then reassembled. "Of course he was. Shame. Though the kids were a bit much. I'm allergic to jam hands. But he was devilishly handsome."

More laughter. Cheryl lapped it up.

The rest of the meeting passed in a blur of notes and nods. Iris said little, scribbled less. Her head buzzed with things she didn't want to feel. She should be used to it—women like Cheryl always commanded attention. They were stars around which others orbited.

But the way she'd said it, so flippant. Like Rafi was another name to pencil in, another heart to prod and shelve. It stung. More than she wanted to admit. She wasn't sure who she was more cross with—Cheryl, Ralph, Rafi, or herself.

By the time the meeting ended, the sun had come out fully, bouncing off the glass windows of the reception like it meant to taunt her. She stepped outside and took a long breath, the salt-tinged air cooling her throat.

She wouldn't cry over linen rotas and women like Cheryl. But she needed to get away from the lodges. Even if just for a few hours.

She whistled for Moss and headed for the path toward the dunes, needing the sea more than she dared admit.

CHAPTER 27: SALTED TRUTHS.

Iris

The coast path unfolded in front of her, winding through the tall grasses and dappled scrub of the dunes, each step softening the knot behind her ribs. Iris knew this route by heart, but it still managed to surprise her—the way it opened out suddenly, offering the full sweep of the Towans' golden sands like a secret laid bare. Three miles of low tide shimmer and hush, the kind of stretch that slowed even the busiest mind.

Moss trotted ahead, nose down, tail swishing, his energy renewed by the scent of salt and rabbit trails. Iris let herself breathe, finally, the kind of breath that reached her shoulders and made her chest ache in a good way. But peace was short-lived.

Moss barked once, sharply, and then took off at a gallop, disappearing over a rise in the dunes.

"Moss!" she called, already jogging after him.

By the time she crested the dune, she spotted him halfway down the slope, nose deep in a crumpled paper bag and tongue working its way through what looked suspiciously like a stolen croissant.

"Moss! No!"

She slipped her way down the sand, mortified, already pulling out an apology.

"I'm so sorry, he's usually better than—"

She stopped. Rafi. Sitting cross-legged on a picnic blanket, camera at his side, takeaway coffee steaming beside him. A second croissant—the untouched one—sat lopsided on a napkin. He looked up slowly, blinking against the sun.

"Of course," she said bitterly. "Waiting for Cheryl, are you?"

His brows lifted. "Excuse me?"

She folded her arms. "She made quite the show this morning. Thought you might have planned a beach brunch."

"Iris—"

"Don't. It's fine. Really. She's got Ralph. She's got you. Apparently it's a lucky summer."

Rafi stood slowly. "You think I'm here for Cheryl?"

She didn't answer. The air between them vibrated with things neither of them wanted to say. Moss, sensing the mood, backed off with what remained of the croissant, tail drooping.

Rafi exhaled. "You think I didn't see how you looked at Ralph? At Lowen Cove."

She blinked. "What?"

"It wasn't Cheryl you were watching."

Iris looked away, arms tightening. "I thought Ralph was different. That he saw me. But I was wrong. He's the same as everyone else. Easy smile, easy promises."

Rafi rubbed a hand across his mouth, something flickering behind his eyes. "Yeah. I know the type."

There was a silence then. Not empty—just waiting.

"Saskia was like that," he said finally. "Sharp. Beautiful. Everyone wanted to be near her. She collected people like trophies. I thought... I thought I was different. But I was just next."

Iris looked at him. Really looked.

"And Cheryl?"

He gave a dry laugh. "A pattern, maybe. Or a moment of

trying to prove something. But I didn't want her. Not really. And definitely not now."

The wind tugged at the edges of the blanket. The sea sighed below them.

"I'm tired of being misunderstood," she said.

"Me too," he replied.

They stood in silence, side by side now, not touching but close. The kind of quiet that asked nothing, but offered everything.

Moss barked once in the distance. A gull cried above. And something, just slightly, shifted.

CHAPTER 28: THE SPACE BETWEEN.

Rafi

He'd woken early. Earlier than usual, even for here. The wind had been quiet when he'd stepped outside, the light barely risen above the dunes, and for once he hadn't reached for his camera. Instead, he'd walked slowly through the morning hush, listening to the whisper of the sea in the distance, the first stirrings of birds in the gorse bushes, the gentle sigh of the world waking up. He'd stood at the edge of the sand, inhaling the scent of salt and something almost sweet—wild fennel, maybe—and let himself feel still for the first time in days.

He'd packed two takeaway coffees and a pair of still-warm croissants from the bakery van that parked in the layby on Thursdays. A peace offering. A hopeful gesture. It had taken effort, this small act, but the idea had rooted itself the night before and refused to let go. He needed to try. To undo what he'd done with his silence.

He knew she surfed early. Iris. It was part of her rhythm, as much as the cleaning rota or Moss's enthusiastic tail wag. He'd watched her come back from it once, windswept and freckled, glowing with a kind of tired happiness he didn't understand but wanted to. She had looked like she belonged to the morning itself—untouched by the clutter of the world.

So he set out to find her, to offer something small and warm and uncomplicated. To try again. Except she wasn't there. The beach was wide and empty, apart from a gull picking at a torn crisp packet and the early shimmer of sunlight on the waves. The tide was out, revealing long flat stretches of sand that glistened like glass, flecked with shells and ribbons of seaweed. He stood there for a moment, coffees in hand, before lowering himself to the sand with a sigh. Spread the blanket. Waited. And with waiting came remembering.

He replayed the night before, the words unsaid, the look in her eyes as she climbed out of the Land Rover. His silence. His clipped goodbye. He'd meant to say something more, something better. But the sting of seeing Cheryl with Ralph had pulled him into old habits. Shut down. Retreat. Defend. That bitterness, sharp and reflexive, had seeped into the moment and turned it cold.

It had felt so much like Saskia. The same way Saskia had glided effortlessly from one connection to the next, always with an audience, always adored. And him, fumbling behind, caught between admiration and ache. She'd broken him down by degrees—not in loud, obvious ways, but in how she made him feel peripheral. And he had let it happen, believing he had to earn his place. That to love her meant to accept her distance, her attention turned elsewhere.

And Cheryl had triggered that same reflex. Just long enough for him to mistake attention for affection. But it wasn't Cheryl he wanted. It had never been Cheryl.

He thought of Iris now. The way she bent to collect sea glass with reverence. The way her laugh felt like part of the tide. How her face caught the light like no one else's, all freckle and sincerity. She wasn't polished. She wasn't performative. She was real. And somehow, that terrified him more. But the fear was starting to lose its edge.

He looked around at the beach, the broad sweep of sand, the endless curl of the sea, the dunes rising behind him like folded arms. This place had worked its way into him, not loudly, not insistently, but gradually. The way salt lingers on skin. The way wind reshapes the edges of stone. He had come here to escape, but now it felt like somewhere to return to.

He was beginning to realise he wanted to leave. Not the lodges or the beach, but the life he'd carried in London—that curated, high-gloss version of himself. The studio bookings. The soulless commissions. The endless performance. Here, in Cornwall, he had let the mask slip, and Iris had seen him. Not flinched. Not turned away. He wanted to stay. Really stay. And he wanted her to know.

The croissants had grown cold, but he left them on the

blanket anyway. He watched the waves roll in, long and lazy, each one curling like a breath. Until the thud of paws in the sand startled him.

Moss. And then her.

Exactly as he'd hoped, though nothing like he'd expected. Her voice was sharp at first, biting in its assumption. Cheryl. Of course she thought he was waiting for Cheryl. Of course she thought the worst.

And yet, they'd found their way through it. Words came. Hard ones, true ones. Her truth. His. Now, as they stood close but not quite touching, the blanket between them rippling faintly in the wind, he felt the ache ease. Just slightly. Maybe they were both a little bruised. A little wary. But in that space between silence and speech, something had softened. And it felt a lot like hope.

CHAPTER 29: WHAT THE TIDE BRINGS IN.

Iris

They tood for a while longer, the quiet between them carrying more weight than anything either of them could say. The sea stretched out like a breath held just beneath the surface, gulls wheeling lazily overhead. Moss had taken up a watchful post at the edge of the blanket, licking his paws and pretending not to listen.

Iris turned her face toward the horizon, the wind tugging gently at her hair. She thought of her grandparents, Ronald and Joyce, and the photo that hung beside her fireplace. The way they stood in it—arms around each other, laughing with a kind of unguarded joy. They hadn't waited for certainty. They had chosen each other, had chosen this place, had built something small and real that lasted.

Courage, Joyce always said in the notes she used to tuck inside birthday cards. Not grand, sweeping bravery—just the quiet kind that told the truth.

"Would you..." Iris started, then faltered.

Rafi turned to her, patient.

She tried again. "Would you want to see something? My art. I mean, it's not really art-art, just... things I make."

His brow lifted, surprised but not mocking. "I'd love to."

She laughed softly, almost nervously. "Don't expect much. It's just shells and sea glass and bits of driftwood."

But even as she said it, she thought of Tom's voice in her head. The way he'd stood in her cottage just a few days earlier, looking at her latest piece with something like pride.

"You always did have an eye, Sis. This is more than decoration. This is you." Maybe it was time someone else saw it too.

They walked back together, not saying much, letting the tide and the sky fill the space between words. When they reached her cottage, she led him inside, heart thudding as she moved toward the corner where her workbench sat beneath the window. She uncovered a few of her latest pieces—a framed panel of sea glass, the colours catching the light like stained glass; a sculpture made from bleached driftwood and tangled fishing line; a mirror rimmed with smooth stones and scallop shells.

Rafi didn't speak at first. He just looked. Not with polite interest, but the intense, thoughtful focus she had seen him use when framing a photograph. Like he was looking through it. Into it.

"This is... beautiful," he said finally, voice quieter now. "It's grounded. It's wild and careful at the same time. It feels like this place, and like you."

She flushed, unsure how to hold the compliment. But her chest expanded, something tight loosening.

And then he stepped forward. The kiss started soft. Gentle. A question. Her fingers curled into his shirt, his hands lifting to her waist. But it deepened quickly, something electric sparking between them, urgent and searching. Her breath caught. She leaned into him, into the safety of it, the thrill of it.

Until his phone rang. He broke away, breath ragged, and pulled the device from his pocket without thinking, glancing down and answering out of habit.

"Hello?"

A beat. Then his face changed.

"Saskia."

Iris froze.

His jaw tightened. "No, I told you. I needed space."

A pause. Then a stream of sharp, bitter sound filled the room. Her name hissed like a blade. Accusations. Cruelty. He ended the call without another word, but the damage hung in the air like static.

"I... I'm sorry," he said. "I need to deal with this. It's not what you think."

She nodded. Tried to believe him. He touched her arm gently, then left. She didn't follow.

Later, needing fresh air and distraction, she walked to the reception to pick up her shift rota. But through the wide glass window, she saw Rafi inside—talking to Cheryl.

They stood close, heads together, flipping through brochures. Cheryl leaned in, a hand brushing his forearm. Iris didn't go in. She turned around and walked home, her heart pounding, heat crawling up her neck.

Foolish. That's what she felt. Foolish for opening the door to something that had never really been hers to begin with.

CHAPTER 30: ALL THE RIGHT REASONS.

Rafi

The walk back to his lodge felt heavier than it should have, like each step pulled a little more weight than the last. The wind had picked up over the dunes, bringing with it the tang of salt and something cooler, like coming rain. His boots sank into the sandy track, and the silence pressed in around him, but it was the kind he needed now—not suffocating, just cleansing.

Once inside, he shut the door with a dull thud, the sound seeming to echo through the small space. He stood in the centre of the lodge, staring down at the phone in his hand. Saskia's name was still lit up from the last call, her voice still echoing in his ears—that familiar mix of accusation, manipulation, and carefully curated cruelty. It used to disarm him. Now it exhausted him.

He sat heavily on the edge of the bed, thumb hovering for a moment before tapping out a message. This isn't healthy. I'm done. Please don't contact me again. He hit send, blocked the number, and set the phone down beside him.

The air in the room shifted. It was strange, the weight that lifted with something so small. A thread finally severed.

He rose, paced a few steps, then stopped. Cheryl. That needed resolving too. He had been careless, and though nothing had happened, it hadn't been fair. Not to her. And not to himself.

He threw on a jacket and headed toward reception, boots striking purpose into the path beneath him.

Cheryl was behind the desk, mid-laugh with another staff member, her polished nails tapping a takeaway coffee cup. She looked up when he walked in, and the shift in her expression was immediate—a flicker of hope tucked beneath her composed smile.

"Hey," he said quietly. "Can we talk for a moment?"

She led him to the corner of the reception with a curious tilt of her head, leaning against the low windowsill.

He didn't hesitate. "I wanted to be clear. I'm not in a place for anything... personal right now. I didn't mean to give the wrong impression. If I did, I'm sorry."

Her lips pressed into a thin smile, the kind that had been trained, perfected. "It's fine," she said breezily. "Summer romances, right? Never last much past the tan lines."

He didn't reply to that. There was nothing to say. It hadn't been a romance. Not even close. He turned to go, then paused.

"Actually... I wanted to ask. What are the options for extending a stay? I'm thinking long-term."

Her eyebrows lifted, caught off guard. "How long are we talking?"

"Six months to start," he said. "Maybe longer. I want to find a place. Something permanent."

She blinked, recovered, and pulled a brochure from under the counter. They went through the options, rates, contracts. Within twenty minutes, the paperwork was signed. Just like that, he wasn't a guest anymore. He was building something.

He stepped out into the light, the wind tugging at his jacket, the path ahead of him brighter somehow. It wasn't just that the coast was beautiful. It was that it felt honest. Every part of this place seemed to strip him back to the essentials—who he was when no one was looking.

Back at the lodge, he opened his laptop, pulled up the folder of images he'd been editing late into the evenings, and attached them to an email for Jules.

Subject: Cornish Gold.

He hit send, not expecting anything immediate. But minutes later, her name flashed up with a reply.

Where the hell has this version of you been hiding? These are your best shots in years. You've got your spark back. Don't lose it.

He leaned back, staring at the message, then looked out through the window at the ribbon of coast in the distance.

No, he wouldn't lose it.

He left the lodge with renewed purpose, heart light and feet quick over the familiar track that led toward her cottage. Each step carried something stronger than nerves. This time, he wasn't coming with apologies or second guesses. He was coming with something clear, something he should have said days ago.

He was staying. And he was ready to begin. With Iris.

CHAPTER 31: FINDING LOVE BETWEEN THE TOWANS.

Iris

The cottage was unusually quiet. Not the comforting kind of quiet that came after a long walk or a storm, but the heavy, waiting kind—like something needed to happen. Iris sat by the window, staring out at the dunes, one hand idly stroking Moss's head. Her art supplies were still spread across the table, but she hadn't touched them. Not since that morning. Not since the moment had been broken.

She'd gone over it in her head too many times. The kiss. The call. The sharpness of Saskia's voice. And then, hours later, Rafi and Cheryl together, heads close, smiling over brochures. That had stuck, stung. She'd felt silly. Exposed. Like she'd cracked open a door only to have it slammed in her face.

So when the knock came, sharp and certain against the wooden frame, her whole body tensed. She opened the door to find him there, breathless from the walk, wind in his hair, a look in his eyes she hadn't seen before—not exactly. Determined. Soft, but certain.

"Enjoy your cosy chat with Cheryl?" she said, more bitterly than intended.

He didn't flinch.

"Very much," he said evenly. "It helped solidify my future with you."

She blinked. "Excuse me?"

He stepped forward slightly. "I told her I wasn't interested. Not in her. Not in anything but you. And then I booked the lodge. Six months. Maybe more. I want to buy somewhere. I want to stay."

There was a silence. Not awkward, but thick with surprise. With shifting ground.

He went on. "This place has done something to me, Iris. And so have you. I can't go back to who I was. I don't want to."

Her eyes were wide, searching his face for a catch, a

shadow. There wasn't one.

She stepped back and let him in. What happened next unfolded gently at first. A glance. A touch. The kind of kiss that says everything you haven't yet found words for. His hands were in her hair, her arms looped around his neck, and then it was no longer gentle.

It was need. It was the ache of having waited too long. Their bodies met like puzzle pieces, as though the time apart had been a mistake they were both desperate to correct.

They made their way to the bedroom without words, shedding years of doubt with every breath and kiss and sigh. Clothes fell away like sea-worn fabric, forgotten on the edge of the bed. Skin met skin. The world quieted around them.

When it was over, or at least paused, they lay tangled together beneath the duvet, breath slowing, limbs heavy and warm. The window was open, letting in the hush of sea wind and the golden spill of early evening.

Iris rested her head against his chest, his fingers lazily tracing her arm.

"You're really staying?" she murmured.

He looked at her, brushing a curl from her cheek. "I'm really staying. If you'll have me."

She smiled, soft and full.

"Then we begin again," she said.

He kissed her shoulder, and they turned their faces toward the dunes, the light softening into something new. And for the first time in a long time, neither of them felt like running.

Later, after tea and toast shared in the kitchen, after laughter had softened all the edges of their earlier confessions, they sat cross-legged on the floor of her tiny lounge surrounded by scraps of sea glass, photographs, driftwood, and prints. Their art lay between them like pages of a shared language. Rafi held one of her pieces—a mosaic of green glass and white shell mounted on slate—and turned it in his hands as if it were something sacred.

"We could do something together," he said. "Your textures. My images."

She looked at him, her heart full. "A show in St Ives?"

"A show in St Ives," he echoed, eyes lit with possibility.

When the sun climbed higher, they changed into wetsuits, laughter following them down the path that led through the dunes. Rafi fumbled with the zip while Iris showed him how to carry the board, grinning at his determination.

At the shoreline, she reached for his hand.

"Time to learn," she said.

He nodded, smiling. "I trust you."

They ran into the surf, boards in hand, water curling around their knees, the sky above a perfect stretch of summer blue.

Together, they headed out toward the breakwater, the sea glinting with light, the wind in their hair, and the laughter of something just beginning.

They had found love between the Towans.

And this was only the start.

ACKNOWLEDGEMENT

To my wonderful husband and daughter—my absolute rocks. Thank you for your unwavering support, love, and laughter, and for enjoying the beauty of the Cornwall coastline as much as I do.

This book grew from a seed of an idea during our shared love for this special part of Cornwall—the golden sands, the wild dunes, and the surf that never disappoints. Our holidays, dune lodge stays, and quiet moments in windswept campsites have shaped every page.

Thank you for breathing it all in with me and helping me form this book—the hours writing, the endless cups of tea, and your patience when I tucked myself away as an idea took hold.

We're lucky enough to live in the beautiful county of Cornwall, with its rugged moors, dramatic coastlines, and stories etched into every tide and path. It is a constant source of inspiration.

This is only the beginning of the Towans series—a

celebration of second chances, slow mornings, and the love stories born where land meets sea. There's something about this place that captures hearts. It certainly captured mine.

I hope to revisit and capture the stories of some of the other characters we've met along the way, continuing soon with the next book: Beneath the Towans Sky.

Printed in Dunstable, United Kingdom

79506680R00087